# Praise for the work of I

"Ramos vividly and affectionately po
Mexican-American heritage and culture."
—*Publishers Weekly* on *My Bad*

"Manuel Ramos is one of my all-time favorite authors and in *My Bad* he delivers everything I look for in a noir tale. Gus Corral is the guy I want on my side if I'm in trouble and Ramos proves once again he is the master of creating great characters. Clear your schedule and be prepared to read this blitz attack of noir in one sitting."
—Jon Jordan, *Crimespree Magazine,* on *My Bad*

"Ramos explores issues of the border, identity, violence and slights from outside the community, as well as within. They are thought-provoking and unpredictable. Many linger long after they end; and often they contain depth charges that explode in the reader's mind after the story has ended. His novels belong on your bookshelves."
—*Los Angeles Review of Books* on *The Skull of Pancho Villa and Other Stories*

"Manuel Ramos has a well-earned reputation for writing gritty stories about Latinos, stories that grab you by the throat. The richness of Ramos' work is evident in *The Skull of Pancho Villa and Other Stories*. The stories are clever and sometimes funny, but their real strength is the way they capture today's Latinos—the talk and humor, the swagger and irony. Ramos has a rich voice. He nails it."
—*The Denver Post* on *The Skull of Pancho Villa and Other Stories*

"Ramos puts Latinos back in the picture. He is known as a crime writer, but that doesn't quite capture what he does. His books are love stories, political dramas, mordant cautionary tales. Characters who are Latino, black and white, artists, professionals and laborers, are described in staccato chapters, like a catchy corrido."
—*Los Angeles Times* on *The Skull of Pancho Villa and Other Stories*

"The Godfather of Chicano noir hits us hard with this collection. Great range, dark visions and lots of mojo—much of it bad to the bone. A fine book!"    —Luis Alberto Urrea, author of *Into the Beautiful North,* on *The Skull of Pancho Villa and Other Stories*

"As invigorating as a dip in a Rocky Mountain stream."
—*Mystery Scene* on *Desperado: A Mile High Noir*

"A dark mix of North Denver gangsters and Catholicism, but it's [the] setting that really grips readers. Nostalgia is combined with reality . . . Ramos gets it right." —*Denver Post* on *Desperado: A Mile High Noir*

"Manuel Ramos captures Denver's Latino North Side in the same intense way that Walter Mosley depicts black L.A. It's all here in a gripping dark mystery: the gritty landscape, the racial tension, the conflict between native and newcomer, the violence and gangs and street loyalties as strong as family ties. No outsider could write about North Denver with such feeling and understanding. A startling novel."
—Sandra Dallas, *New York Times* best-selling author, on *Desperado: A Mile High Noir*

"Manuel Ramos has taken the best elements of classic noir—the loser anti-hero, urban grittiness, thuggish cops and femme fatales, double and triple crosses—and updated them for the age of Obama. Money, sex and greed figure prominently in the story but so do class tensions, barrio culture and a multicultural milieu. Ramos handles all of these elements with a deft hand that keeps the story moving and, while avoiding any overt messaging, creates an up-to-the-minute portrait of the new America. I loved this book!"
—Michael Nava, author of the Henry Rios Mystery series, on *Desperado: A Mile High Noir*

"A very impressive debut."
—*Los Angeles Times* on *The Ballad of Rocky Ruiz*

"A thickly atmospheric first novel—with just enough mystery to hold together a powerfully elegiac memoir of the heady early days of Chicano activism." —*Kirkus Reviews* on *The Ballad of Rocky Ruiz*

"Ramos succeeds brilliantly in marrying style and substance to form a seamlessly entertaining novel [with] characters and scenes deeply etched with admirable brevity and skill."
—*Publishers Weekly,* starred review, on *Blues for the Buffalo*

# THE GOLDEN HAVANA NIGHT

*A Sherlock Homie Mystery*

## Manuel Ramos

Arte Público Press
Houston, Texas

*The Golden Havana Night: A Sherlock Homie Mystery* is funded in part by a grant from the the National Endowment for the Arts. We are grateful for their support.

*Recovering the past, creating the future*

Arte Público Press
University of Houston
4902 Gulf Fwy, Bldg 19, Rm 100
Houston, Texas 77204-2004


Cover design by Mora Des!gn


Names: Ramos, Manuel, author.
Title: The Golden Havana Night : a Sherlock Homie Mystery /
    Manuel Ramos.
Description: Houston, TX : Arte Público Press, [2018]
Identifiers: LCCN 2018030391 (print) I LCCN 2018033261 (ebook) I
    ISBN 9781518505409 (ePub) I ISBN 9781518505416 (Kindle) I
    ISBN 9781518505423 (pdf) I ISBN 9781558858671 (alk. paper)
Subjects: I GSAFD: Mystery fiction.
Classification: LCC PS3568.A4468 (ebook) I LCC PS3568.A4468 G65
    2018 (print) I DDC 813/.54—dc23
LC record available at https://lccn.loc.gov/2018030391


♾ The paper used in this publication meets the requirements of the American National Standard for Information Sciences—Permanence of Paper for Printed Library Materials, ANSI Z39.48-1984.

18 19 20 21          5 4 3 2 1

*For my mother, Emma.*

*Thank you, Flo, my co-conspirator.*

He knew he'd killed another dream but must
accept the consequences.
　　　　　　　—Leonardo Padura, *Havana Blue*


There is nothing tougher than a tough Mexican, just as there is
nothing gentler than a gentle Mexican, nothing more honest
than an honest Mexican, and above all nothing
sadder than a sad Mexican.
　　　　　　　—Philip Marlowe, private investigator,
　　　　　　　in Raymond Chandler's *The Long Goodbye*

# PROLOGUE

He shivered in the cold Colorado morning. The sun was but a pale ball in the gray sky. It provided little warmth. He blew stale air on his hands.

Weather was an illusion. He knew the difference between illusion and the real. Real surrounded him: the rifle, his plan, the details that had to work for him to move forward. His commitment. As real as it gets.

He'd scouted the shot when he could. Not every day, but enough. It had taken time, but he had plenty of that. More than he needed.

He leaned once more into his Barrett M82, and sighted it to the spot on the highway where the target would stop. The weapon was ready. He believed he was, too.

From his position on the rise, he had clear sight to the entrance ramp. Every minute, more traffic rushed through the entrance to merge with the southbound lanes of I-25. The oblivious commuters had no idea they were only extras in the scene he directed. They couldn't imagine, much less experience, the emotions he stored and which were about to be released with justice and penance.

The homeless beggar, his unwitting accomplice, would walk through the traffic to his place near the top of the ramp. The homeless man broke the law by standing there, and each time he did, he brought the wave of cars, trucks and vans to a sudden slowdown. The police would eventually take him away, but he would return the next day or the day after. The pattern had been established. It was what the shooter needed.

The target invariably slowed down as he waited his turn to drive around the panhandler, the scene was always the same, and at the same time—between seven and seven thirty-five. The metallic red E300 Mercedes would stop, the target would shake his head, curse the beggar. But no matter how many times the beggar stalled him, the target used the same route from his house to his office. Every morning, like clockwork.

There were other variables, tiny things that could go wrong and keep him from pulling the trigger. Had to be textbook. He waited for the right shot, the right time. The *perfect* time. He'd passed up two opportunities already; he might again if he didn't feel good about the shot.

The red car pulled into the lane to catch I-25 South.

The beggar's dirty fingers gripped a cardboard sign. His hands were half-covered with raggedy mittens. Today the sign read, "Any kindness will help. God Bless You."

The target inched forward, stopped.

The shooter adjusted his scope, breathed.

The target's head was centered. He smoked a cigarette this morning in the luxury of his automobile. His chin bounced to the rhythm of whatever nonsense he listened to on his radio.

From experience, the shooter knew that only that chin and lower jaw would remain connected to the target's body after the bullet did its work.

The shooter felt the calm overtake him. He'd done this far too many times to doubt that he would succeed.

He caressed the gun, squeezed the trigger in sync with his breath. He prepared for the recoil by relaxing even more.

In the blink of an eye, red explosion bloomed inside the car— that and a splatter on the windshield. The shooter watched the Mercedes jerk forward into the rear of the car at the head of the line. He gave himself just a split second to confirm, to savor, then began moving mechanically; he broke down the weapon, packed his gear, slung the canvas bag over his shoulder. He slipped away while horns honked on the street below. He scurried to the bike path and walked a mile before he stopped.

He'd done it. He felt good, successful.

Next, he would find Corrine Coral and bring it all to an end. He hoped Gus wouldn't interfere. He'd deal with him, if necessary.

For the first time in a long time he was complete. Justified. At peace.

# Part One

# - Chapter 1 -
## THE HOOCHIE COOCHIE MAN

Joaquín "Kino" Machaco didn't have an appointment but that didn't stop the all-star center fielder for the Colorado Rockies from coming through the door and planting himself right in front of me. He leaned in, knuckles resting on my desk, his jaw tight. I couldn't see anything in my office except the bulk of his chest and the shiny sweat on his face.

The brass plaque on the office door said, *Agustín Corral—Investigator*. Agustín is my given name, but to any and all I was Gus. That day, Gus was the unwelcome focus of Kino Machaco's undivided attention.

"I got a problem," he said. "A personal problem. I heard you were the guy to help me."

The ballplayer loomed over me like a gorilla about to smash a termite nest. I pushed back my chair to open breathing space between us.

"Sit down. Let's talk. Maybe I can help. Maybe not."

His eyes moved left and right as though my words were nonsense.

"Why wouldn't you help me?"

It wasn't really a question. More like a warning.

"I didn't say that. Easy. Sit down. Let's talk. Tell me about your problem."

Kino sat down with a thud. The reupholstered chair groaned under his weight. I'd found the chair at Goodwill and replaced one of the legs as well as the ripped fabric. Kino could put a quick end to the chair's newly revived life.

"I don't know if I can help," I said. "That's all I'm saying. I usually work for lawyers—sometimes they use me like an investigator, but I can clean windows and throw out the trash,

3

too." I gave him my *howdy, new customer* grin, but he continued to glare at me. I replaced my wasted smile with a look that was all-business.

"Like a utility player? Pinch-hitter, maybe?"

Machaco's Cuban accent played with my ears. I heard "peench-heeter." He occasionally lapsed into Spanish, and the accent clung to each of his English words, but he was sincere and convincing, not at all what I expected. The smooth swing that ESPN highlighted almost every week was matched by his smooth style of talking, smiling and dressing. *Suave*, as my neighborhood pals used to say.

The man's neat beard covered the lower half of his face. The top of his head was a glistening bronze globe of naked skin. The famous tattooed forearms, responsible for hitting at least forty homers during a half-dozen seasons, rested across his chest, but his fingers and hands moved constantly.

Almost ten years before, Kino Machaco had defected from Cuba to play ball in the United States. He was a teenager when he made his move. At the time, the story ran for several days, especially the part about his sprint through the Washington, D.C. airport to a waiting car that sped through a rainy night to the U.S. Embassy. After the legal maneuvers stopped and Fidel Castro was somehow compensated and the headlines quieted down, the Colorado Rockies tied him up with a truckload of money and a tightly written, long-term contract. He spent a year and a half in the minors, then made a big splash in his major league debut. *Rookie of the Year*, as I remembered. *Savior of the Woeful Rockies*, for sure, and at last.

I picked up a pen and was about to ask him some basic questions when he said, "The lawyer, the old guy, retired. He said you could help. Never mind you're not a lawyer. That's why I'm here."

I'd thought as much. My pal Luis Móntez had sent another client my way. His last two referrals never paid their bills, and one tried to beat me up. Kino Machaco had money. At least that was an improvement.

"He must have told you all I do is simple stuff. I haven't had my investigator's license very long."

"*Sí, me dijo.* I don't need no detective. Don't need no license. I need someone who can help."

He looked me over like I was a prize hog at the state fair and he was the grill master at a BBQ joint.

I straightened my posture and stretched my chest. "With what? Let's start there."

He finally quit moving his hands. He stared over my shoulder and out my solitary office window at the beautiful view of the overflowing alley dumpster.

"You never say nothing about this to no one, okay?"

I nodded. "It's confidential," I said. "Unless you tell me you're gonna rob a bank or kill someone."

He jerked his head back in my direction.

"I ain't robbing a bank. Or killing no one."

"Just tell me what your problem is."

The chair made a noise like a tree limb breaking as he stood up and paced around my crowded office.

"I live with my brother here in the States," he said. "My only family in this country. He's got a special visa so he's not illegal. The team, the Rockies, they handled my brother's paperwork and other legal stuff so I could focus on playing ball. I'd be all alone if Alberto wasn't here."

"I get it."

"So, it's important that he be here."

"Sure, I understand."

"But not if it means he could get hurt."

"Is someone threatening him?"

He stopped his aimless walking and went back to looking at the alley *basura.* He nodded. "Yeah. I been getting messages, through my sister back on the island. There's a guy, a bad guy. Miguel Almeida. He's telling her that Alberto owes him money and that if he doesn't take care of his debt, something's going to happen. Something bad."

"To your brother? Or you?"

He shrugged. He clasped his hands together and raised them over his head. "Maybe me. Maybe Alberto. Or my sister, Lourdes."

He sat down again. The chair wobbled, and Kino grabbed the edge of my desk to steady himself. "I just . . . I just don't know," he said.

"Is the threat that serious to you if he's in Cuba and you're here? In the States?"

He muttered something I couldn't hear.

"What did you say?"

He straightened his back. "I said, this guy could hurt any one of us, whenever he wants. He has business in Florida, and connections in New York. He could come for me wherever he wants."

Spring training was set to start in another week. Kino Machaco wouldn't have his head in the game if he thought his brother or his sister, or he himself, was someone's target. How could he play ball if he worried about who sat in the stands?

"Don't you have to leave for Arizona? Most of the team is already down in Scottsdale, aren't they?"

I could take or leave Denver professional sports. I'd occasionally watch a Broncos game with my sister Corrine or a few old friends, especially if the team was in the playoffs, but, unlike thousands of Denver football freaks, I didn't stroke out if they lost to the Raiders or they couldn't find a solid quarterback. Nuggets? I could do without. Avalanche? What was it they played again? Rockies? I'd been to a few games with the lawyer, Móntez, who had a love-hate thing with that team.

I did read the sports pages almost every day. Not because I was a fanatic, but because those pages always had stories right out of a soap opera or *telenovela*: drugs, divorces, assaults, betrayals, health crises and the occasional poor boy or girl makes good. Pure entertainment. My kind of reading. But if it was up to me only, I could think of plenty of other ways to spend the sizable chunk of change it cost to watch millionaires make more millions playing children's games while they generated even many more millions for the team owners, league bosses and TV executives.

Still, even I knew that Kino Machaco was something special in the world of professional baseball. If he wasn't getting ready for the upcoming season, plenty of well-heeled team owners, TV execs, sporting goods CEOs and other one-percenters would sweat blood counting potential lost revenue as Kino and I talked about his family problems with a Cuban gangster.

"Yes," Kino said, "I should be in camp. But I can't think about baseball. Alberto's hiding out, more or less. He won't leave our house, won't travel to Arizona with me like he always does. But I should be in camp. This has to be fixed. Before something happens."

Several different thoughts tried to connect, each one making my skull draw tighter around the feeling that the more I learned about Kino's "personal problem," the deeper I fell into a hole of obligation to the super jock. And I didn't have a good history of climbing out of holes.

"When you say 'something bad' is going to happen, what do you mean? Is your brother's life in danger? Do you need to talk to the police?"

His eyes narrowed, and his gaze focused on the space between my eyes. I felt like a curve ball that didn't break, waiting for the swing of his bat to knock me over the left field fence.

"You're a smart man, Gus. It's obvious. And I talked with people about you. You speak like an educated person, carry yourself with confidence, which impresses me because I know your history."

He had my attention.

"Plenty of time to read in prison," I said. "That was where I got my education."

"I know that. You overcame that, used it. That's why I can talk to you about things that maybe a less intelligent man might not appreciate. *¿Entiendes?*"

"Whatever, man."

He frowned but continued. "I can't get mixed up in this business with Almeida, officially. But here's the truth . . . " He hesitated, eyes on mine. "No one else hears about this?"

"Yeah, I got it."

"My brother gambles. There are times he has no control. He bets on everything. He was that way when he was a boy and he sold numbers for *la bolita*, the lottery. It was illegal, sure. Castro outlawed the game, called it counter-revolutionary. But Alberto took the risk. Eventually, he made bets with his customers."

He waved his arms as though he could shake off his brother's screw-ups. "He thinks he will always win. Now, he owes this man several thousands of dollars for bets he lost."

"How much?"

"Half a million dollars."

I made a sound that must've been a groan or a whimper. That was a lot of money.

"If I'm connected to that, I could get thrown out of baseball. I can't risk the police. And I can't pay off the debts. Alberto has to do that."

"He has that kind of money?"

"He's my partner in a few businesses. He can get his hands on the money, especially if I don't get in his way."

He meant that he would give his brother the money, but he couldn't say it.

According to a recent newspaper profile about the star player, Kino Machaco was a heavy investor in Denver real estate. He had to have options for the kind of money the Rockies paid him and those options apparently meant opportunity for the brother. Kino made his brother a rich man, but he still needed to bail Alberto out of trouble with his bookie.

"I don't want to call the police," he continued. "They couldn't do anything to Almeida. I want you, or someone, to fix this. Almeida has to leave my brother alone. That's what has to happen."

The tightening skin around my forehead was joined by warning bells that echoed against my eardrums. I'd become an investigator more out of necessity than choice. It's no news flash that ex-cons weren't usually at the top of the list of likely-to-be-hired, no matter what the job might be. I thought I was good at what I did; a bit more experience and I'd be excellent, I told myself on those days when no one called, no one stopped by the office.

I'd grown up on the Northside of Denver, where I'd perfected survival skills—skills that came in handy on some of my less
glamorous jobs. Old habits die hard. I tried to ignore the internal
alarm by telling myself that I had to let go of my prison paranoia
and not always assume the worst about people, or the messes they
brought to me. I needed their troubles to make a living. I carried
on with my questions.

"Well, if your brother can get the money, why won't he pay?
Or, you could give the money to your brother, then let him pay
off his debts. Isn't that the easiest solution?"

"Yes, of course. I . . . uh . . . I'm just worried that if I'm
involved in any way, no matter how small, my career is over. I
don't want to touch the money. Baseball is very nervous these
days about gambling."

*As well as performance-enhancing drugs and domestic violence,*
I thought. "Other guys have been suspended or thrown out for
stuff you'd never expect would be a problem. I love my brother,
but I have to be careful."

"He bet on your games? Maybe on you?"

He nodded.

"Yes. He made stupid bets that could cause me trouble." He
again thumped his fist on my desk. "But that's not the reason I
want to make this go away."

"It's a good enough reason."

"Maybe. But it could be dangerous for Alberto. This man
doesn't like him. He hates our entire family. Alberto says that
some of the debts are from years ago, and Almeida accused him
of running away to avoid paying. He could hurt Alberto, even if
he's paid. But if you're with him, he won't do anything. He won't
touch a messenger who has money, especially if the messenger is
from the States."

"He kept taking your brother's bets, even though he wasn't
getting paid?"

"Yes. I think he wanted to get him in as deep as he could,
and . . ."

"What else?"

"And sometimes Alberto used other names, or other people to make the bets. But now . . . "

"Almeida knows the truth?"

"Yes."

"And you want me to carry the money to pay him off?"

"My brother has to make the payoff, even though he's afraid. I told him he must go. He has to make this right. But someone should be with him. To hold the cash."

"Hold up. Why not just transfer the money from your brother's bank to a bank in Havana? Why does someone have to actually deliver the money?"

He shook his head.

"Cuba and the U.S. don't have that kind of system in place. Not yet. It's still not that open. And Almeida can't risk that his business gets out in public. Even if we could set up a bank transfer, he wouldn't go for it. What he does is illegal, and you don't want to be caught doing anything illegal in Castro's Cuba. No, the money has to be handed over face-to-face."

"That's what I'll do?"

"Yeah, sure. That, and you will also be with Alberto for protection, and to make sure Hoochie gets the message that he can't do anything to my brother. Or me."

"Hoochie?"

"That's what they call him."

"What kind of name is that?"

"His name's Miguel Almeida, like I said. But when he was a boy his family lived for about a year in New Orleans. His father, Jorge Martínez Almeida, was on Castro's payroll, although he said he worked for a Mexican company. The story's always been that during his time as a spy he passed himself off as a businessman, and he used his family for cover. The kid got the nickname around then: *Hoochie Coochie Man* becuase he worked as a bouncer in a strip club . . . or a whorehouse. Who knows? Might have been both. He was only sixteen or seventeen, but he was big and tough."

I wrote down everything he said, including Hoochie Coochie.

"These days," he said, "he's just Hoochie. He's been back on the island for years, but he still uses that damn nickname."

How bad could the man be if he called himself *Hoochie*? Almeida must have thought the name was strong or cool or intimidating or whatever, and that was enough. Things like common sense and reality pulled no weight against what people wanted to hear and believe.

I didn't say anything about the nickname. "One thing I don't get."

"What's that?" he asked.

"This guy, Almeida, sounds like he's got a major operation in place. But, *in Cuba*? No disrespect, but isn't it a poor country? Very poor? People have money for gambling on that scale? Small bets, I understand, but for something like what you describe, there'd have to be a lot of money floating around. Is that what's happening?"

He shook his finger at me, as though I were a kid talking out of turn.

"It's complicated, sure. But even in Cuba, where things have been controlled for years, there are people who have more than others. People who still live in fancy houses, who hire maids and drivers, who make decisions for others. They have money, or the power to get money. And some of them use that money for things the government would never approve. Almeida survives because of these people, and he has become rich because of their illegal activities."

I pushed ahead.

"You want me to tag along with your brother, to carry the cash, then watch the payoff and make sure nothing goes screwy. That about it?"

"Yeah, that's most of it."

His words hung in the air, but he didn't offer to explain what else there was.

"Let me guess," I said. "Not only do I protect your brother from this Hoochie guy, but maybe I protect Alberto, and the money, from Alberto himself? Five hundred grand will be a big temptation for a man with a gambling problem. That part of the job, too?"

He started to say something, but the words wouldn't come out. He nodded.

"This will be an expensive job," I said.

"I'll pay for what needs to be done. Not a problem."

"Yeah, I believe it. But even though it's easier to get into Cuba, there's still a few hoops we have to go through. How soon does this have to happen?"

I tripped out on the idea that Cuba might be just what I needed, especially if someone else was paying for the ride: get away from the cold, miserable blasts of the dying Colorado winter. Stretch out on a beach, eat *arroz con pollo* and kick back with a rum concoction or two. Maybe commingle with the locals over a set of Latin jazz even, or a more traditional *son*. And all I had to do was make sure a Cuban bad guy didn't hurt the brother of a baseball superstar while a payment of a pile of overdue money was made to that same bad guy—money that somehow would make its way into the island fortress of Cuba. And this only, if I could keep the brother away from the Miami racetrack or the underground floating Havana poker game in the meantime. That's all.

"It has to be done quickly," Kino said. He sounded out-of-breath. "In the next few weeks."

And just like that, the Cuban beach sunk into the mire of my muddy alley, and my *arroz con pollo* turned into another Burger King Whopper.

"I don't think that can happen. I need time."

"What's the problem?" Kino asked. "You need a passport? Or can't you travel out of Colorado?"

"No, I've got a passport. But I have responsibilities to my clients. I can't just leave my business. I'm barely making it now. I have standing obligations to various clients that need attention. If I don't follow through, my future as an investigator won't be too profitable. Give me a month, no problem." I paused for a heartbeat. I didn't want to say it, but I had no choice: "You better find someone else."

He didn't look fazed by my words. He shook his head.

"No, you're the guy. I know guys like you, from the street. You're my man. You'll be paid very well and if this works out, I'll send you more business than you can handle. Many clients." He surveyed my drab office. "Important clients."

I thought all the clients I had were important, but I let it slide. "You talking about the Rockies?"

"No, not the Rockies. People who owe me favors, who want to help me. They do what they can to make my life here in the States as comfortable as it can be. Sometimes they need the kind of help I think you can give them." He rubbed his shaved head with a slow circular motion. "Ben Sardo, my agent, from L.A.," he added, as though that explained everything. "He will contact you soon. Today. He's in Denver, closing a deal for office space. He will be a good resource for you and can take care of the papers and travel arrangements. He's okay. He saved me when I came to the States."

This guy really wanted me to work for him. I had to wonder, *Why me?* But I didn't ask that question. The answer might've killed the deal.

"I guess I don't have a lot of time to pack."

Kino stretched his hand to me and I grabbed it. When he finally let go, he smiled. He turned to walk out of my office, then he twisted back to me.

"There's one more thing you should probably know."

I shook the blood back into my fingers. "What's that?"

"I killed Hoochie's brother before I left Cuba. That's still a thing with him."

# - Chapter 2 -
## LA IGLESIA DE BOXEO

Kino returned to the chair and told me his story. He spoke quietly, sometimes barely above a whisper. At times, he closed his eyes.

He began with a simple statement: "Boxing in Cuba is a religion, not a sport."

I believed him. From what I knew of Cuban fascination with the sweet science, faithful throngs worshipped before the god of jabs and hooks, and they prayed for miracles. Their prayers were often answered; although professional boxing was officially outlawed, amateur fighters brought glory to Cuba. Cuban teams won more international matches than any other country, including gold medals in the Olympics. Holding up his family's tradition, Kino Machaco was baptized into the *iglesia de boxeo* at the age of twelve, when he started lessons and training at the Rafael Trejo gym in Havana.

"I was big and strong," he said, pride creeping into his accent. "I could knock down fighters twice my age. My feet were fast. The legendary Julio Mateo was my trainer, and he was part of the team that developed another legend, Félix Savón, Ninote. Everyone said I could be as good as him, if I kept at it. And I did, for years. But I didn't love boxing. I loved baseball."

He executed a muscle-bound shrug, and baby elephants crawled across his shoulders.

"I had to be angry when I boxed. Mateo said, again and again, that if I wasn't mad, I would be hurt. He preached that without *coraje*, I was just another poor Cuban boy waiting to have his brains, and all sense, knocked out."

His hands folded into fists. I don't think he noticed.

"I believed him and that's how I fought. It became part of me. Mateo taught me to fight with anger, *coraje, pasión.* I learned the

14

lesson well—I had to. Boxing was fire and stone fists and lightning moves."

He unclenched his fists and spread his fingers along the front edge of my desk.

"I didn't have to be mad to play baseball. I just had to play. Baseball is like . . . like a river in a valley, flowing to the sea."

He looked away, embarrassed, I assumed, by his poetic description of the sport that had made him a millionaire several times over.

The sports pages consistently carried stories of Machaco's generosity. Reporters often commented on his "softer" side: his friendship with Latino writers and musicians, his commitment to causes such as cultural museums and art exhibits, his frequent visits to children's hospitals. The super jock appeared to have more going for him than brainless athletic skill.

"That's where you met this Hoochie character?" I asked.

"He was a few years older. He and his brother hung around the gym, but only Claudio, the younger brother, worked out. Hoochie was too busy trying to impress the girls, or running an angle on a mark, or betting on the matches our trainers set up. He was that way as a boy—a manipulator, an operator, and he stayed that way as a man."

I nodded because I knew the type of man he described. At one point in my life, I would have fit the description.

"We all wanted to be picked for the national team, for the chance to fight in the Pan Am Games, even the Olympics. *Entonces*, most of us ignored Hoochie and his shady business. We were too busy, training hard."

"You fought Claudio? Is that how he died?"

He folded his arms in front of his chest.

"We fought, yes, but it was his brother who wanted the match. He drilled into Claudio that he was the next champ, the next Cuban hero. He knew that a fight with me could jump start Claudio's career. I didn't want to do it. I was bigger, better. Everyone knew that, but Hoochie wouldn't let it go. Finally, one very hot day when I was fed up with Hoochie's constant challenges and taunts, and even Mateo was tired of his bragging and loud talk, we told him we would do it. I was mad enough to fight, just like I'd been trained."

"Why would Claudio agree? Did he think he could win a match with you?"

His head jerked rapidly, left and right. "He knew. He knew he had no chance. But he couldn't resist his brother. He imitated his swagger and his talk and his attitude." He paused, and it was obvious he debated with himself about what he would say next. "And there was a girl."

"Someone you both wanted?"

He nodded. "Marita. We called her Marí. Both Claudio and I competed for her. I think, now that I understand what was happening, that the fight would never have happened, even with Hoochie's interference, except for Marita Valdés. She kept us both at bay, and yet . . . "

He stopped talking, shook his head and stood up again. "I have to go. I've spent too much time here. Ben will contact you."

I grabbed his wrist. He twisted away, easily.

"I'm not doing anything until I hear all that's gone on between you and this Hoochie guy. How and why did you kill his brother?"

He stared at me for a long ten seconds. He licked his lips. "It was a brutal, bloody fight that convinced me I could never be a boxer." He sat down again.

"Claudio was smaller than me, but faster. I cut his eye early in the fight, and he bled like a hog with its throat cut. But he wouldn't quit, wouldn't go down. He used his speed to his advantage, and after a few rounds my ribs were bruised and my face was as bloody as his. Marí watched from the front row, and I thought she screamed for me. Claudio must have thought she cheered for him. Mateo wanted to stop the fight but Hoochie, acting like his brother's trainer, insisted that we continue. He had bet money on the fight, a lot of money."

I looked closer at his face. Faint slivers of scar tissue lined his cheeks and the skin around his eyes.

"At the beginning of the ninth round, the fight was finally stopped. We were carried away, bloody and exhausted. Claudio was in terrible shape. I won, according to Mateo but we both ended up in the hospital. I didn't feel like a winner."

"Hoochie lost his bets?"

"Of course not. He bet that his brother would lose, but that he'd last at least eight rounds. That's why he wouldn't let Claudio stop. He needed him to make it through the eighth round. Hoochie was the only real winner that day."

I jumped to another conclusion. "But that's not how Claudio died."

"No, he didn't die from that fight. Not directly."

He shrugged his massive shoulders again.

"I was checking out of the hospital. It was two nights after the fight, late. My brother was with me. Claudio was leaving at the same time. When we were outside, I tried to shake his hand. I wanted to show him that I had no hard feelings about the fight. He walked away, ignoring me. That's when we saw Hoochie and Marí. She sat with him in his beat-up car, and it was all obvious. I wasn't surprised; kind of expected it, if you want to know the truth. But Claudio . . . he lost it. He went after his brother."

"He brought her to the hospital, where you both could see her?"

"Sure, what the hell did he care? He was rolling in money. He had Marí. He wanted to show her off. *And* he expected Claudio to accept it."

"Claudio fought Hoochie?"

"He tried to. He ran to the car, jerked open the door and reached for his brother. Hoochie backed up the car, laughing at all of us, but especially at his brother. Marí, too—she laughed as hard as he did. Hoochie reversed in jerks, making the car jump . . . all the time laughing. Claudio was out of his mind."

He stopped talking. He breathed in, long and hard.

"I could see that he was going to get hurt. Claudio's face cuts started to bleed, and each time he went after Hoochie and Marita, Hoochie made the car jump, nearly hitting Claudio. I hollered at him, but he kept at it. I grabbed him by the arms and pulled him back to the sidewalk. But I couldn't control him. *Estaba loco, loco.*"

"This was outside the hospital?"

"We had moved up the street. By then we were out of the light. The night made it hard for us to see unless we were close to the headlight beams. They were dim and flickered, but Hoochie continued to tease his brother."

"It was only you, Alberto and Claudio in the street, and Hoochie and Marita in the car?"

Kino rubbed his hands over his face. "Yes, yes. I shouted for Claudio to stop, that they weren't worth the pain. He swung his arms and hit me in the face. I reacted by hitting him in the stomach, hard. *Demasiado duro.* He spun around, clutching his belly. I tried to grab him again, but he fell backwards into the street, still holding his gut. He was hit by a car we hadn't noticed in the scuffle. The force of the impact knocked him over the hood. He died on the ground, not ten yards from his brother."

"The police? What did they do?"

"They concluded it was an accident, which was the truth. If anyone was to blame it was Hoochie, but because of his father's government connections he was untouchable."

"But he laid the blame on you?"

"*Claro.* He came after me that night, and later. For a couple of years, I had to defend myself, watch for him, until I finally left Havana. He made my life miserable. He and his thugs tried to catch me alone, but I stayed one step ahead of them even though I could take care of myself if I had to."

"You were playing ball by then?"

"Yes. If it hadn't been for baseball . . . no telling what I might've done. I was in the spotlight, so Hoochie had to leave me alone. There were always reporters and government officials around me. I protected myself by staying in the spotlight, where everyone could see me. But when I had the chance to play ball in the States, I jumped at it. Ben Sardo and his partners got word to me in Cuba, and the rest, my escape to this country, my contract—you know all about it, I'm sure. After that, I didn't hear about him. Nothing. Until now that my brother has had his own trouble with Hoochie Almeida."

"With all that history, why would your brother have any contact with him?"

"He has a sickness, *una enfermedad,* and nothing else matters when it takes hold. Hoochie probably cheated him, took advantage."

His eyes clouded. Pity for his brother? Regret? Anger? Frustration? In the few minutes we'd been talking, I realized that Kino Machaco was a complex man. He had all the swagger and ego of any other rich jock making a living in the United States, but there was something else to the man. I couldn't put my finger on it then. I watched him move around my office as soft and agile as a cat, strong, maybe even invulnerable. But his eyes burned with the passion created by his brother's troubles. His voice cracked at times. At other times he appeared desperate and in a hurry. The sports writers called him a clubhouse leader, even though he was a quiet player—the player everyone listened to when he did speak out.

"Your agent's gonna call me?"

"No. He'll come by. Give him one or two hours. Will he find you here?"

"I'll be here. Looking at maps of Cuba, reading Cuban history and worrying about all the money we have to get into Cuba."

"*Bueno.* He'll have papers for you to sign. Officially you'll be working for my brother, but I'll be your boss."

The negativity that had clung to him only minutes before vanished, replaced with a return to his athletic optimism. He looked like he was ready for a doubleheader. Even his next string of sentences sounded like a pregame pump up session.

"I got confidence in you, my man. You ready for this? We can do this, Gus. You solid?"

My head filled with sports clichés. "No I in team." "Let's play two." "Winning isn't everything, it's the *only* thing." "Wait until next year," or something like that. I thought back to when I played pick-up basketball at the Twentieth Street gym, when I sweated out bone-jarring games that settled testosterone-fueled street rivalries. I got sucked into Kino's vibe, whatever it was.

"Yeah," I said, "I'm solid."

# - Chapter 3 -
## ONLY BUSINESS

I hadn't seen Jerome Rodríguez in several weeks. We'd drifted apart, but I never took the time to figure out why. Over the years, that happened with people I called friends. One day we could be as close as tequila and bad decisions, and then, before I knew what happened, months, sometimes years passed by without any connection. I called it my life.

But the isolation wasn't always because of me and my general anti-social personality—the character flaw that Corrine, my sister, called my "Mexican melancholy." When she first said that phrase, I accused her of reading too many back issues of *White Woman's World* at Gloria's Glam House and Pedicure Palace. She socked my bicep so hard I felt it in my toes.

Several chums and buddies from B.P. (before prison) didn't look me up when I was released, and with others I eventually realized that we'd grown up and whatever bond we'd made at North High School had worn out, along with our yearbooks and letterman jackets.

Jerome was different. We'd met when we both were going through major life changes, and those early days together cemented a true alliance. But he had to be wary of his friendship with me. We'd been through some gritty times together, and the grit was all my fault. The ex-homeless vet, jailbird and now successful small business owner had stuck with me when hoodlums and crazy men shot at us, kidnapped us and generally made our lives miserable—or tried to end them altogether. Like the lucky penny, though, Jerome turned up when I needed him the most.

I called him and asked if he could stop by. I told him I was working for the superstar, Joaquín Machaco, and I wanted to pick his brain. He mumbled something that sounded like an "okay," and then he hung up.

I looked through the *Denver Post* while I waited for Jerome. Whoever had the office before me must have paid for a long-term subscription. Each morning a paper waited for me, leaning against the office door, and each morning I amused myself with the sports pages and, occasionally, the Life & Culture section for the crossword puzzle.

That morning my attention was grabbed by a front-page headline that announced the sixth shooting on I-25, the main Colorado freeway that sliced the state in two, north to south. Apparently random travelers, anywhere along the highway, were targets for a shooter who used a .22 pistol to take pot shots at drivers. One woman had been killed, and two men seriously injured when they were shot at and lost control of their cars. Three others had bullet holes in their windshields. Accounts differed about the possible car the shooter drove: a blue Chevy pickup with Wyoming plates, a gray and green late-model Subaru, a van with blacked out windows. I made a mental note to stay off I-25 until the serial shooter was arrested. Then I turned to the crossword.

Jerome showed up about an hour later. He wore a bright yellow cap that sported the logo for the local jazz station, a dark blue shiny workout T-shirt and faded jeans. For the first time I noticed wrinkles around his eyes and sagging flesh at his throat. I'd never thought of it before, but Jerome was at least fifteen years older than me, maybe twenty. He'd always been in top shape, and his age had been irrelevant in the craziness we'd shared in the past. Now I sensed that the years were finally catching up to him.

"Hey, bud. Long time . . . "

"Yeah," he answered.

He plopped down in the chair. He looked tired, sad even. I offered him a bottle of water and then we both stared at our hands for a minute or two.

"What the hell does Kino Machaco want from *you*?" he asked when the silence became obvious. "He's really your client?"

"Sure, why not? He needs someone who can be discreet."

Jerome rolled his eyes.

"Don't worry. No trouble for you. I promise."

"Of course, I don't believe you. At least he can pay your bill."

"That's good, right?"

"It's different, I'll give you that."

"Machaco could help build my business."

"You're serious about this detective gig? I never would have guessed that for you. The Northside homie makes good, eh? The little Latin shamus. A regular *Sherlock Homie*."

He chuckled at his play on words.

"Maybe I'll hang a sign on the door—*Sherlock Homie: Detective, Because Crime Does Not Pay Unless You're A Dick*."

We laughed, and for a moment it felt like old times. Then he slipped back into his darkness.

"What's up, Jerome?"

He hesitated. This was a Jerome I didn't recognize: uneasy, subdued. He stretched his left arm out in front of him and held it straight at eye level. His fingers and hand quivered like a branch in the wind.

"See that?"

"Yeah, what is it?"

"I've had the tremor for about a year. Lately it's gotten worse. The doctor is convinced it's Parkinson's, so . . . guess it is. I thought I should tell someone. Turned out to be you."

I'd never known Jerome to be sick, not so much as a hangover in our time together. The news was tough to get a handle on. I struggled to say something that wouldn't sound phony or stupid.

"I don't know much about that disease. What does it mean for you?"

"They tell me it's different for everyone, except we all get worse, though some more than others. Eventually, I'll get meds for the symptoms that interfere with life, like the tremor. There's no cure. I could end up in a wheelchair, unable to keep my balance. Maybe my brain slows down, and then . . ." He shrugged.

"Right now, what it means is that I should exercise, every day if possible. Denver has a lot of classes and resources for people with Parkinson's. I'm going to be in the best shape of my life. Except for the shakes."

Jerome had always been direct, cold even. The way he described his illness made it sound as though he were talking about someone else, a distant relative maybe, who had a strange and unwelcome condition but who, in the long run, would not intrude into Jerome's life.

"But maybe it's manageable, right? Doesn't have to end up with you on your back?"

"Yeah. Maybe."

"You need help with something? Anything I can do?"

"No. I only told you because the doc thinks my family and friends should be aware, just in case I start having more severe symptoms. These days, Gus, whether you like it or not, you are both my friend and my family. Now I've told you. We can move on."

Jerome's news set me back for a minute. How was I supposed to act towards him now? As soon as I had that thought, I knew that's what he didn't want—for me to change the way I thought about him or the way I acted around him. The way I treated him had to stay the same.

When I first met Jerome, he was a homeless drifter. He sold me old 45 records that he insisted were rare and collectible. He'd been in war and in prison. When he found his footing, he turned into a successful hustler who profited off the rapid erasure of the Denver where I had grown up and the transformation of my hometown into something I still hadn't figured out. Jerome adapted. I returned to him again and again when I needed the kind of help that I couldn't advertise for in the usual places. I wondered how much of the Jerome I knew would change into someone else.

"Okay, we'll move on," I said. "But you ever need anything, you got my number."

"Yeah, you bet."

He looked away and stuck his hands in his pockets.

I gave him the whore's bath version of my latest job. His frown turned uglier the more I talked.

"You get busted in Cuba, you're dead meat," he finally said. "That's not bullshit, you understand?"

I nodded.

"You'll be paraded on Cuban TV as a Yankee spy and the U.S. won't even know your name."

"All I have to do is supervise the transfer of the money. I'm not smuggling it into Cuba, not even going to touch it."

I wasn't sure about that, but it sounded good.

Jerome was about to point out how wrong I was when the office door swung open, cutting him off in mid-critique. My one-room office suddenly felt tiny and crowded. The guy standing in the doorway oozed money and slick charm, expensive clothes and even more expensive vices. His precise haircut, pearl cufflinks and a slight hint of mint and lime told me he was the kind of guy who always seemed to have a drink in his hand at parties but who never got drunk, the kind of guy who drove a tricked-out sports car but never got a ticket. A hard-to-like kind of guy.

He held a dark brown soft leather briefcase that he set on the floor. I'd never had a positive experience with a man who carried a briefcase.

"Corral?" he asked, with a perfect Spanish pronunciation of my name. "I'm . . . "

"Ben Sardo," I interrupted.

He nodded and extended his hand. I took it, and introduced Jerome as my friend and occasional business associate. Sardo smiled a ten-thousand-watt smile and pulled up the remaining chair.

"No offense," he said, "but I assume we can talk freely here with Jerome?"

His smile jumped up a couple more thousand watts.

"Actually," Jerome said, "I should go. You can make this mistake on your own, Sherlock."

"You can stay," I offered.

He stood up, a trace of awkwardness in his movements. He shook his head and was gone before I could come up with a good reason for him to stick around.

"I hope your friend is all right," Sardo said. "I didn't mean to offend."

"Don't sweat it. Jerome's okay, he just doesn't make a good first impression. That's all."

"I know people who are the same way." He twisted in the chair like he'd sat on something wet.

"The other chair's more comfortable," I said.

He waved me off. "No problem." Then to business. "Kino explained the circumstances? You're good with what we need to do?"

"The basics are clear, but I have a few questions."

"No doubt, that's why I'm here. Shoot."

"Why me? Kino can afford to hire anyone in the country. Top agencies, with a lot of resources. I'm not exactly a household name when it comes to private investigators. And it's not like I have any special knowledge about Cuba. Again: why me?"

He leaned back in his chair.

"I'm gonna level with you, Gus. Hope you don't mind. And if you don't like what I say, you can back out. After all, it's only business. Nothing's in stone between you and Kino, or you and I for that matter. Not yet."

"I got it."

"Frankly, at the beginning, Kino wasn't sure about you. Your lawyer friend, Móntez, recommended you, and Kino thinks Móntez is the best. Móntez helped him out a few years ago when a gold-digger with greedy fingers grabbed what she thought was her ticket to ride. He solved it quickly and, what's more important, quietly. A real stand-up guy—trustworthy, loyal. Those things are important to Kino. He'd rather trust someone like your lawyer than any high-priced firm. In many ways, he's still running in the Havana streets, true to his roots."

"Good to know," I said.

"So . . . based on Móntez's recommendation, he had you checked and decided to give you a look-see, to feel you out—take your temperature, if you know what I mean. He was still wary."

"His visit today was to audition me?"

"Something like that. Whatever it was, now you're Kino's guy. I guess he liked this office, or your attitude, or the way you handled his story about his brother and the boxing match. You passed. I admit I myself don't understand it, and I gave him other names and referrals, but he's my client *and* my friend and I usually go along with what he wants."

A loose, out-of-place thread on the collar of his soft-looking shirt jiggled as he spoke. The thread tainted the impression he worked hard to create.

He quit smiling. "You need to grasp one thing. I am very protective of both my clients and my friends. Like I said, Kino is both. You do anything that might harm him, and I'll cut you off at the knees." He wiggled his index finger at me. "You got that, right?"

He wasn't the same flim-flam man who'd walked into my office. He'd changed like a snake dropping his dead skin. The fact that he threatened me in my own office made it clear that now he was something else, something darker around the edges, maybe even dangerous. For an instant I thought about what he might do if I crossed him, but only for an instant. His client wanted me and that was enough. Whatever show he thought he had to put on, whatever game the agent wanted to play, he could do without my participation—or my worry.

"It's all good, Ben," I said. "There's nothing I can do that will harm Kino Machaco, and we both want it that way. Kino came to me, remember? If you walk out now, my life doesn't change. Neither good or bad. If you stay, I'll do the best I can for your man. Guaranteed."

The edginess left him, and the glib salesman was back. "Your next question?" he asked.

"How's the money getting into Cuba?"

"You probably shouldn't know. Not that anything illegal is planned, but there are people involved, here and in Cuba, who don't appreciate a spotlight on their affairs. Any of their affairs. Kino is important to these people, so they go out of their way to accommodate him. Helping him feel secure about his brother is all part of protecting their investment. They will take care of the money, at least as far as delivering it to the island."

I didn't believe for a second that nothing illegal was planned. "We'll pick it up in Cuba?"

"The money will be waiting for you and Alberto when you land in Havana. Lourdes Rivera, Kino's sister, will have it."

"If Alberto has that kind of money, why not pay his bets? Why all this trouble if money is not the issue?"

Sardo moved forward in his seat. Again, he looked uncomfortable. I made a note to replace the chair.

"The money's not your concern, other than making sure it gets delivered. Kino does a lot for his brother: allows him in on his business, looks after him, but that's because Alberto helps Kino in many ways. That's all you need to know about that."

"I might need to know more about that, actually, but that's enough for now."

Without realizing it, I had become a participant in a weird game with Sardo. Every word had two meanings, every shrug was a message, every eye blink was a sign, a tell. I wondered if all high-end agents, managers and other parasites who made money from someone else's talent were like Ben Sardo.

"The sister meets us at the airport, with the money. Then what?"

"She will set up the meet with Almeida. You transport the money to him, make sure he's fully aware that his days of threatening the Machaco family are over and then you return to Denver. Or spend a few days enjoying the sights if that's what you're into. There shouldn't be any trouble. Although, and I'm pretty sure you know this, Hoochie might need convincing that he can't take any more bets from Alberto. You believe that nickname? Crazy, right?"

"Yeah, crazy. How much convincing is expected from me?"

He grinned, and his shiny white teeth beamed at me like a lighthouse in the fog.

"Kino expects this payoff to end his troubles with Hoochie. That's your job: end this. You're a big boy, been around, did time. I know about you and I don't think you're a babe in the woods. That's one reason I went along with Kino when he said he wanted you to handle this. Do what you have to so that Kino never has to worry about his brother's gambling problem in Cuba again."

I knew exactly what he meant but I wanted to test him. "Within reason, right?"

"Of course, of course." He was a little too quick with his response. "Within reason. Nothing too outrageous, Gus. We're civilized men and Kino can't be involved in anything over the line."

The words sounded as sincere as a billionaire president promising to fulfill the dreams of the poor middle class.

He stood up, looked around my pathetic office, shrugged, and then smiled at me. I was really getting tired of his smile.

"Just make sure it's over, Gus. Absolutely over."

His smile went away again. His faded blue eyes bored into me, and I had to look away. He pulled a bulky clasp-and-string envelope out of his briefcase.

"Here's a contract you should sign. Says you're working for A&M Enterprises, one of Alberto's companies. You're finalizing a business arrangement with the honorable Miguel Almeida, Cuban businessman. You also have to sign a few papers so your trip to Cuba is legal. Nothing too difficult. You'll be paid twenty-five grand when you return from Cuba with a successful completion of your project. Plus, all your expenses are paid or will be reimbursed. There's two grand in the envelope to get you started. Get what you think you'll need for the job. This money doesn't count against your twenty-five thousand."

He handed the envelope to me. I undid the string, spread the money and contract pages on my desk.

"Be ready to leave day after tomorrow. You're booked on a seven a.m. flight to Los Angeles. You'll meet Alberto there. Then the two of you fly nonstop to Havana. Before you ask—it's easier this way; there are no nonstops to Havana from Denver, and the flights to Cuba from DIA are a lot longer than five hours. Once in Havana Lourdes will have instructions for you."

He was strictly business. Serious and focused. I'd seen three different Ben Sardos in the short time of his visit. First, the slick, fast-talking con man. Then the menacing, edgy enforcer. Finally, the no-nonsense agent, efficiently and professionally wrapping up loose ends for his client. I wondered how many other Ben Sardos existed, and how many I would confront before my latest job ended. And if I'd ever meet the real Ben Sardo.

# - Chapter 4 -
## NO ENCHILADAS

I braced for a lecture from Corrine when I stopped by her house to tell her about my upcoming trip. Corrine was the oldest in the family: age-wise, I was stuck between her and my younger sister Maxine, so, of course, she thought she knew what was best for me and how I should live my life. She was usually right, but I'd never admit that—not directly anyway.

I'd said it before. I loved my sisters, both of them. Corrine and Maxine were rock solid in their own ways. Max was married to the love of her life, Sandra, and together they made waves in the Colorado music scene with their band, Mezcla. Corrine was a historic figure in the Denver Latino community. If there was a protest, petition or press conference happening, Corrine was there. She was a hard act to follow, so I didn't try.

And she was a total pain in the butt.

She told me once that I was the smartest in the family, the one with the most promise, but that I'd wasted my life and brought embarrassment to the family name. Believe it or not, she was trying to be nice and supportive when she said that.

While I walked to her front door I practiced in my head the possible responses to her resistance. I had quick comebacks and wise-ass quips ready for her. I didn't have a good logical explanation, other than the caper was a good-paying job, but money had never impressed Corrine.

She opened the door and immediately retreated to the kitchen.

"Back here," she hollered. "I'm making something for tomorrow's potluck at the rec center. There's coffee."

I smelled bubbling, red chile sauce. I was in luck, I figured, thinking a late lunch was in the picture. I sat down at her kitchen table and drank the small cup of very strong espresso she had served me. She moved gracefully from her stove to the counter to the sink and back to the stove. I explained my new job and waited for her reaction.

Her eyebrows turned up and I braced myself. A quick instant of disapproval or maybe ridicule passed across her face. Then, the eyebrows relaxed.

"I'm jealous," she said. "I want to visit Cuba before Starbucks ruins it for everybody."

The purpose behind my travel plans didn't seem to matter to her.

"That's all?" I asked, underwhelmed by her words.

She shrugged. "I've given up trying to understand you, Gus. You're a grown man. You want to play footsies with these people and dare the Cuban government to lock your ass up, that's totally on you."

I guess I'd expected her to talk me out of the job. She was my compass, my guide. If she didn't care anymore, I was in trouble.

"Maybe I can get you a ticket—if you want to tag along."

I was only half-joking.

She sprinkled chopped onion on a tray of enchiladas as she talked. My stomach rumbled, my nose twitched and my mouth watered.

She shook her head. "No way. I'd love to see Havana, talk with the Cuban people. But not on this mission. When you get arrested—and you will get arrested—you'll have to deal with the embassy. They'll want a contact in the States, someone to vouch for you, someone who can verify your crazy story, whatever it is." She paused. "Don't use my name."

She looked up from the food to emphasize her words, then wiped her hands on a dish towel and tossed it on the counter. She slid the tray into her oven and shut the oven door, a little too forcefully, I thought.

I finished the coffee, said a quick goodbye and left. She didn't offer me any enchiladas. Corrine was pissed, and in a way I hadn't seen before. Now *I* was worried.

৩» ৩» ৩»

I spent the night reading everything I could find on the Internet about Kino Machaco and Cuba. There was a lot.

I read baseball stories, Cuban restaurant reviews, travel tips and Kino's Wikipedia page, complete with photographs of him as a child—a large child—in Cuba. I learned about his many business ventures and the good work of his charitable foundation, KinoKare Unlimited, dedicated to education progress in Latin America.

I surprised myself when I stumbled on an article about the chef and restaurant owner Miguel Almeida, one of the "more successful capitalist entrepreneurs in the new Cuba," who was "leading the charge into an open and vibrant Cuban economy." No mention of his nickname.

I found very little about the rest of Machaco's family, other than minimal mentions that he had a younger brother and an older sister.

I fell asleep at the computer. About two in the morning I woke up, downed a shot of tequila and stumbled to my bedroom.

I dreamed I was on a leaky raft with Jerome. Sea water collected around my feet. Sharks bumped the raft and tried to ram their heads through the bottom. The sun reflected off the water and blinded me. I felt the raft slipping away. I no longer saw Jerome, but I heard Corrine laughing. The ocean rolled over me. I smelled enchilada sauce. Then I woke up.

Most mornings, I forgot my dreams as soon as I opened my eyes. If I did remember any part of a dream, I never dwelled on the nonsense my brain had created while I slept. This raft dream, though, just wouldn't let go. I retained details, like shark teeth and Jerome's flip-flops. The colors were vivid.

I didn't like the idea that a dream might actually mean something. I shook it off. I concluded that the dream was a creature of my upcoming trip to Cuba, of my conversation with Jerome, my disappointment at Corrine's failure to feed me and the cheap tequila I drank before I hit the sack. Nothing more.

I hurried through my morning routine. I felt as though I didn't have enough time for everything I had to do before Cuba.

When I got to my office, a man waited in the dimness of the narrow hallway. He looked as though he'd had a hard night and looked even more like it was just another stacked at the top of a hard life. A thin shabby overcoat draped across sloping shoulders. The cuffs of shiny pants dragged at the back of worn and muddy sneakers. At least three days of beard darkened his face. Bloodshot eyes blinked through dirty glasses.

I'd come to the office to tie up some loose ends before Cuba. I planned to let clients know I'd be out of touch for several days but that I'd be back to wrap up whatever it was they hired me to do for them. Despite what I'd told Kino, none of them had anything urgent. Most were divorce lawyers who wanted papers served for hearings weeks away, or background information on the opposing parties or—surprise—on their own clients. Nothing that couldn't be put on hold for a couple of weeks.

"Gus Corral?" the overcoat man asked. His bruised voice sounded hollow in the empty lobby.

His face squared up at me and I knew what he was going to say. I spoke first. "Sorry, buddy. I'm leaving town. I can't take on any new clients right now. Come back in ten days or so."

His lower lip trembled slightly. I couldn't think of what need a guy on the skids would have for a private detective. I pitied him a bit until I realized he wasn't going anywhere. He shifted his weight from one leg to the other and stood quietly in the hallway while I unlocked the office door. He was as tall as me but not as heavy. He looked tough. A hard character. I watched him over my shoulder, fearful that he would try something behind my back, or that he might have a weapon.

As I turned the key I told myself to knock it off. It hadn't been that long ago that his wardrobe and general scruffy appearance would have fit me to a T. I thought, *Where's your compassion, Corral?* I opened the door and was about to shut it in his face, when he rushed past me.

"Hey," I said. "What the hell are you doing?"

He backed into a corner and held his hands up, palms forward. "I'm not any trouble. Honest. I just got something . . . I need to talk with you. Just five minutes. That's all. Honest."

He sounded as though he might start crying, and again I found myself feeling sorry for the guy. But I had to put him off.

"I don't have time. I told you. I'm leaving town. Tomorrow. I have a lot of things to deal with before I can leave. No time for you."

He reached inside his coat. I tensed and readied myself to jump, in one direction or the other.

"Maybe this will help." He held up a plastic bag.

"I don't want any drugs," I said.

"It's not drugs."

I looked closely at the bag and saw that it was filled with money.

"I can pay," he said. "I'll pay you just to talk. I'm not a crook."

He dumped the money on my desk. Most of the bills were twenties but I scanned a few fifties and a couple of hundreds in the pile.

"There's no need for that," I said.

His lip continued to shake.

"You want some water?"

He nodded, then sat down. It seemed like me newly revamped chair was seeing a lot of action lately; it was probably as ready for me to be in Cuba as I was. The man's chin drooped to his chest. I grabbed a bottle of water from the cooler along the wall and handed it to him.

He said, "Thanks," but didn't do anything with the bottle.

I picked up a few of the bills and looked at them closely. They were wrinkled, as though they'd been in the bag for a long time. Several had coffee stains. I gathered the money and put it back in the bag.

"What's your name? Where'd you get this money? What do you want from me?"

"My name's Hudgens. Leo Hudgens." He looked nervous, and as he spoke his words ran over one another like fish trapped in a net. "I'm a cop, was a cop—retired. Might not look like one now. That money's from my savings. I took it out of the bank a long time ago, but I haven't needed it until now. I've been livin' on the street." He searched my office with his eyes. "I've had some problems with . . . uh . . . with booze and my back and painkillers. But I can't put it off any more. I need your help."

"How'd you get my name?"

He blinked his eyes several times before he answered. "Ana Domingo. The Community Liaison Officer over at the Denver PD. I met her when I was on the force. You know her? She said she knew *you*. Said you were the kind of investigator I needed, that you could help. You know her, right?"

Ana had dumped me for a Mexican cop, who then dumped her. It felt like ancient history that I didn't want to resurrect.

"Oh yeah, I know Ana. Kind of surprised she recommended me, but okay, okay."

"I didn't tell her everything. Only that I needed someone who was good and did out-of-the-ordinary jobs. That I needed to find somebody without attracting too much attention. She gave me your name pretty quick."

"Doesn't change the fact that I'm leaving town."

He cleared his throat, then coughed into his fist. His coughing continued for several seconds. He opened the bottle of water and took a long drink.

When he caught his breath and calmed down, he said, barely above a whisper, "Hear me out. Five minutes. Honest."

He drank more water. His fingers shook, badly, and he had to hold the bottle with both hands.

I gave him five minutes, he took twenty.

# - Chapter 5 -
## LEO HUDGENS

"I was a good cop," he began. "But, in the end, that didn't mean anything."

I sat back and listened to the soft-spoken, worn-out man.

"For six years I did my job, honestly and clean. I didn't take any payoffs or bribes. I didn't manhandle suspects, never lost my cool. In the service I was a sniper, and on the force I earned marksman status. I did community work, had friends in the chief's office and in the neighborhoods I worked. You won't believe this, but the mayor knew my name."

I looked at the clock on the wall. He sped up his narrative.

"I was on my way up—I'm tellin' the truth. My life was good. Shit, I had some rough times, especially growing up as one of only a few white kids on my block in Five Points, which, back then, was all-black. Denver's ghetto some called it. But I thought it was okay. That was all in the past. I had a great job and I was in love and engaged."

He finished his bottle of water.

"Something happened," I offered.

He made me nervous. He was down but not quite out. He could say complete sentences and he knew the right words. But his face betrayed a wounded, maybe even desperate man. The face and the words didn't go together.

"About six years ago, Lisa and I planned to get married in the spring." The skin around his eyes wrinkled when he said the woman's name. "That winter, everything changed." He paused, coughed. "It started when my partner retired. Gary Obregón was a legend on the force and he taught me well. When he moved on he told me to remember two things. The only thanks cops should expect is in the paycheck." The words sounded like a prayer. "And the second was that it was easy to cross the line, but almost impossible to cross back. He never told me what he meant by 'the line.'" He turned the empty plastic bottle in his cut and worn hands. "I learned that on my own."

I fished a bottle of water for myself from the cooler and handed him another. He set it on the desk.

"My new partner had a reputation, not a good one. I'd clashed a couple of times with Dominick Alito over the years, over how he handled suspects or witnesses at crime scenes where we both ended up. But for the most part he lived in his version of cop world and I lived in mine. It didn't take long for the problems to bust out."

"He roughed up somebody?" I asked.

"It started with that."

He chugged water, took a deep breath and looked ready to proceed.

"Before you go any further I should warn you," I said. "You're not my client yet, and I'm not working for your attorney. That means I might have to reveal what you tell me if it ever came to that. Be careful what you say."

"You mean like to the police or a district attorney?"

"Yes, exactly. Think about your words."

"I'm at the point where I don't give a damn. I'm gonna tell you what happened. I have to."

"Your decision. Go on then."

"We were patrolling the Park Hill neighborhood, about midnight, when we saw a dented car with two black youths back out of a driveway and tear ass down the street. Alito hollered like he'd won the lottery, swung around and we pulled them over. It was easy to spot. The driver's door was a rusty red, the rest of the car had splotches of gray and black. It looked out of place, especially coming from the driveway of one of those old but well-kept houses in Park Hill. But there wasn't anything specific the boys had done that gave us cause to stop them. Didn't matter to Alito."

I knew what Hudgens talked about. I'd been in the same situation, except I was one of the dark-skinned boys in a beat-up car in a neighborhood where we didn't belong, stopped by suspicious cops on a dark street. That night stayed with me for years.

"We stopped the car near an empty lot and they pulled over where there were no street lights. Bad luck for them. Alito ordered the boys to lay down on the street. He was having a good time. I told him to stop, but he ignored me. He kicked the boys, called them names, generally tried to scare them into admitting that they'd done something illegal back at the house. But the driver, an eighteen-year-old named Delly Thomas, insisted that they had stopped to see a girl who lived in the house, but no one was home. He even gave us the girl's name, told Alito to check out the owner of the house, said it was the girl's father and he gave us his name. Alito didn't even consider doing that. Not for a second."

My mouth dried up and I drank water. My throat tightened as I swallowed. The story hit too close to the bone. I'd lived it, seen it. I knew it too well, could see where it was going but couldn't change it. And all I thought of was punching out Hudgens as he told his story.

"Alito made Thomas stand up and he escorted him back to the squad car. He told me to watch the other kid. 'Keep him on ice,' he said. The second boy, Leon Parker, sixteen, was still on the ground. He'd started to cry when Alito kicked him, but he was quiet when Alito and Thomas disappeared into the darkness. He asked if he could sit up. That's when we heard the knocks and whacks of Alito beating up Delly Thomas. I thought for sure someone else would hear what Alito was doing and he would have to stop. But no one came, no one stopped him. Parker sat up and looked at me, begging me to do something. He twitched with every blow coming from behind the squad car. He cried again, and spit and snot trickled down his chin."

"You didn't try to stop Alito?" I managed to ask.

"No, I did not. I knew what I had to do, I'd been a cop for years. A good cop. Not a spot on my record. I knew, I knew, but I didn't do anything. I just let it play out."

"What happened?" I wanted him to finish and leave my office.

"Alito came out of the dark and headed for us. His hands were bloody and sweat covered his face. The boy I watched, Parker, jumped to his feet. He looked at Alito, then at me. He hesitated, said something like 'Leave me alone,' then took off running. Alito hollered for him to stop, but he kept on. I acted on instinct, on my training. I ran after him and tackled him. We both went flying through the night. We crashed to the pavement. Parker's head bounced on the curb. Blood spurted on my jacket from a crack in his skull."

"You killed him?" My throat constricted, and I had to drink more water.

He nodded.

I couldn't respond. Hudgens' story triggered a vague memory of the boy who'd been killed running from the police. The official version, the accepted version, said that he and his friend had been stopped for a traffic violation. Leon Parker had jumped out of the car when the police approached. Apparently, he panicked because he'd recently been released from the state's Detention Center for Boys and he didn't want to go back. He tripped in the darkness and killed himself when his head smashed on the curb. The boys had been drinking. The other boy, Delly Thomas, had to be subdued with force when he saw what happened to his friend. The two officers involved were cleared by the District Attorney after an appropriate investigation. That official version had nothing to do with the truth but that's how it ended.

"After that," Hudgens said, "Alito had me in his pocket. It started slow: a free meal, an envelope of cash, a bag of dope to make our own sale. He dragged me down to his level. We did every bad and wrong thing cops can do, over and over, again and again, until I quit giving a damn and eventually lost everything—Lisa, my job, my self-respect."

His eyes were dull, not focused on anything.

"What about Delly Thomas?"

"No one believed his version of what happened that night. At least no one who could do anything about it. I kept tabs on him for a while. He drifted from one arrest to another for drugs, petty theft, assault. Last I heard he was in prison for burglary."

"And Alito?"

"He retired, took his pension. Moved out of state, somewhere in California. I lost track of him. That's why I need to hire you."

"I can't work for you," I said. I felt only contempt for Hudgens.

"Okay, not for me. Maybe for Leon Parker and Delly Thomas? Would you work for them?"

"What do you mean?"

"I've spent the last five years living in shit. I put myself in hell and I knew that's where I belonged. Now I see that I have to do something. I can't make it right, but I can tell the truth. It won't bring back Leon Parker, but it might clear his name."

"You can tell the truth, as you put it, without anything from me."

"Yeah, I could. And I'll take whatever consequences happen. There has to be something else. Alito has to know, he has to pay. I want you to find him so I can bring him in when I confess. I want him standing there when I tell the world what really happened to Leon Parker and Delly Thomas." He said the two names in a rush as though the wind had been knocked out of his lungs. He breathed in deeply. "I want you to track down Dominick Alito."

He was a blubbering mess when he finished. His dirty clothes and wasted appearance had polluted my office. The truth of what he'd done contaminated me and I had to stop myself from throwing him through the door.

I breathed deeply, gagged on his body odor and tried to say something that made sense.

"I can't do anything now. I told you that. What's the rush? You've waited five years to come clean. What's another two weeks?"

"Only that I may turn back to the coward I've been for those five years. The longer I wait, the more likely I'll change my mind and disappear again. I've got to do this now. I don't have a lot of time."

Another coughing fit hit him, and I understood that there was a second reason for Hudgens' rush to find justice.

"I can't do it," I repeated. "I can't take on your job now."

His eyes closed, his head drooped.

"But maybe there is something that can be done."

"What's that?"

"I have a friend. A techie. She owes me a favor. I can ask her to look for Alito on her computer. She knows how to do just about anything on a computer. She can do that while I'm gone. If she finds anything, she can contact you. If there's more to it, I'll check it out when I get back."

He didn't do anything that told me he'd heard what I said.

"You got it? Give me a way to contact you, and I'll give it to my friend. Her name's Sofía Santisteven but everyone calls her Soapy."

He shrugged.

"That's all I can do now."

He reached inside his overcoat. He pulled out a pencil and a piece of paper, wrote his name and a number and set it on my desk. He stood up to leave.

"You want some advice?" I asked.

He stared at me like I'd said something stupid.

"Go to the cops and tell them what happened. Don't wait to find Alito. He may never turn up or your story may bring him out, but you shouldn't wait. Go to the cops today."

He stuck his hands in his coat and hunched his shoulders. He nodded. "I'll think about it. You're probably right. Yeah."

He walked out of my office. I tried to ignore the smell in the air and the bad taste in my mouth.

# - Chapter 6 -
## TAKING THE OX BY THE HORNS

LAX overwhelmed me with indistinct noise, conspicuous lights, rushing people and frantic movement. The bright purple suitcase with an orange belt tied around its middle was easy to spot on the baggage carousel. As I grabbed it I tried to convince myself that no one laughed. After all, hundreds of travelers of several colors and nationalities scurried in the baggage claim area, some with luggage that was more laughable than mine; boxes secured with twine, greasy denim sacks, half-opened and ripped plastic suitcases. I acted like I knew what to do and where to go but I had to read Sardo's written instructions again to take the next step after I reclaimed the bag I'd borrowed from Corrine.

I had about an hour before my flight to Havana took off.

I walked around the terminal for several minutes to stretch my legs and clear my head. I hadn't slept well after finishing my internet binge of Kino and useful Cuban information. The truth is, my brain overloaded, and my eyes cramped from the glare of my cheap laptop. Then, during the night, my feet burned with anxiety, and I couldn't decide if I was too hot or too cold. Not only did I have to get up at four a.m. to Lyft to the airport, but the sorry image of Leo Hudgens haunted me. His story of the death of Leon Parker planted itself firmly in my head, and I couldn't shake it. I turned and tossed in frustrating sessions of hazy semi-consciousness, not actual sleep. I'd napped on the plane, but I still felt groggy. My lack of sleep caused an uneasiness in my gut and a sag in my confidence.

Sardo had given me a card that I scanned to open the door to the Alaska Airlines VIP lounge. The small room was packed, but in the crowd of students, families and elderly tourists, I saw my man almost immediately. Alberto Machaco waited at a small table with two cups of coffee and two Danish. He smiled the instant our eyes met, and I returned the smile like we were old friends.

He wore charcoal gray slacks, a tan polo shirt and bright blue running shoes. A pair of sunglasses dangled around his neck on a gold chain. He was dark: black hair, eyebrows and eyes, smooth brown skin. He wasn't as tall as his brother, but his shirt couldn't hide a muscular Machaco chest and toned biceps.

He stood and hugged me, and I hugged back. Maybe we *were* old friends.

"So happy to meet you, Gus," he said. His accent was as thick as Kino's.

"Yeah," I answered. "Same for me."

I hadn't known what to expect, but his relaxed attitude helped me chill. He didn't appear nervous about his upcoming meeting with the infamous Hoochie.

"Were you on the flight from Denver? I didn't see you."

"No, no," he said. "I've been in L. A. for a few days. Business, for me and Joaquín." He pointed to the coffee. "It's not bad. Don't know how you like it so I picked up sugar and cream. I take mine *sin nada, negro*. Black."

"Yeah, black is fine," I said. I pulled myself together and focused on Machaco, him and the reasons I was in the Los Angeles airport in the first place. The bitter spirit of Hudgens finally faded away.

Was this smooth-looking, polished fellow really a gambling addict. A man who had to run back to Cuba to settle his debts, the same man who'd put his brother and sister at risk because he had no self-control when it came to money and odds?

We sat on the soft chairs and he leaned in close.

"I've heard about you from Joaquín," he said. "I am to put my trust in you completely when it comes to how we handle Hoochie. And so, I will." He patted me on the back. "We're in this together, of course, but I am to follow your lead if we get in any . . . uh, uncomfortable situations, shall we say?"

He didn't wink at me but the way he talked gave me that feeling.

"This is pretty serious, right?" I asked. "We get caught with the money in Cuba, and it will raise questions we don't want to answer. And then there's Hoochie. He's dangerous. He's threatened to hurt you or your family. We have to be careful. We have to avoid situations, uncomfortable or not."

He frowned.

"I know all that. I've had to deal with Almeida for years. There's nothing you can say about him that I don't already know."

"Well, maybe you can fill *me* in. Tell me everything you know about him, even if you think I already know it. I don't want to be surprised by anything while I'm on this job. Start at the beginning."

He shrugged, finished his coffee. Then he talked. He worked his way through his family's roots in Havana, Kino's natural athletic ability and how his older brother always looked out for him. Then he gave me the familiar boxing story that Kino had told me, and it was close to the same version. He was adamant that his brother hadn't killed Claudio. "That was that dumb fucker's own fault," he said in Spanish. Not that it seemed to matter. Hoochie had tormented him and Kino for years, until they finally left Cuba.

"And now you're going back, to pay off your debt to a man who blames your brother for *his* brother's death. You sure that's a good idea?"

He started to answer but was interrupted by an intercom announcement that our flight was boarding. I emptied my coffee cup, swallowed my last bit of Danish, and we made our way to the gate. He never answered my question.

๑๛ ๑๛ ๑๛

From my seat on the plane, the José Martí International Airport looked like a set for a low-budget action movie. I imagined the plot featured the latest exploits of a Yankee soldier of fortune planning to outwit the natives and bed the beautiful but secretive

French female scientist. The main blue and yellow buildings looked tired, and the terminal itself wasn't in much better shape.

We walked from the plane towards a doorway in one of the buildings. The tropical smell and humidity hit me immediately. A clear, pure sky surrounded the shimmering sun. Talkative, laughing airport workers unloaded our luggage and piled it on the tarmac. I wondered if the money was in one of those bags. Soldiers carrying automatic rifles signaled for us to speed it up and get inside.

The place was drab, very industrial. The comfort of travelers was obviously not a priority of the bureaucrats who ran the place. The restrooms were a disaster, so unkept I almost didn't use one.

We found the appropriate line and waited.

When we finally moved, young Cubans in olive green uniforms checked our papers and asked perfunctory questions. The men were serious and abrupt. The women had short skirts or pants but could be just as serious as the men. I followed Alberto and did what he did. We waited for several minutes for our luggage until the carousel noisily started up and we grabbed our bags. Before I knew quite what had happened, we were outside the terminal looking for Lourdes Rivera.

I'd made it to Cuba.

Lourdes showed up about fifteen minutes later in a yellow taxi van driven by Carlito, a clean-shaven, pale man wearing black pants and a white shirt. She was dressed in casual clothes but gave the impression that she had several irons in the fire and not much time for her brother and his unlikely companion. The introductions were quick and elementary. She gave Alberto a sisterly hug before they engaged in small talk about the family. She asked about Kino, and Alberto simply said, "*Como siempre*, he doesn't change."

We climbed into the van and began our trek from the airport into the city. Alberto and I sat in the back. Lourdes sat up front, giving directions to Carlito. Her legs straddled a crimson canvas bag. I assumed the money was in the bag and she would give it to us along with our instructions on where and when we were to deal with Hoochie.

The clean van, obviously past its prime, chugged and wheezed at about fifty miles an hour. I guessed that it was Russian, or Eastern European.

Carlito talked a mile a minute to Lourdes. She answered brusquely, sometimes with a snarl, sometimes with a smile. I caught pieces of the conversation, everything from baseball predictions to the lack of vegetables in the city markets to the horrendous condition of the roads.

Cuba rolled past, and I drifted with the green scenery and powder blue skies. Tropical vegetation lined the edge of the highway. There was traffic but nothing like congested Denver. Carlito drove like a pro, never losing much speed as he maneuvered around slow-moving trucks or horse-drawn wagons. He avoided most of the potholes, but occasionally he'd hit one and we'd all jerk and hang onto our seats.

Lourdes looked back from her seat. "About twenty minutes and we'll be at the house where you two are staying. It's in the city, not far from the hospital for foreigners. It's comfortable. But you have to be out in a week. You need to get this business done quickly." She turned without waiting for any response.

Alberto sat next to me, quiet. He stared at his sister. The gladhand, even cheery guy I'd talked with at LAX now sullenly waited for whatever his former home had in store for him.

Wooden shacks and royal palm trees lined the edge of a narrow stretch of highway. Carlito slowed down for a blind curve. As he made the turn I saw a police car parked at an angle to the road. Four men in uniforms stood near the car. One of the men signaled for Carlito to pull over.

"What's this?" Alberto asked. He clutched his briefcase.

"They want to check Carlito's papers," Lourdes answered. "It's nothing. He must show that this is the taxi he's licensed for. Everything's in order. It'll just take a few minutes."

She sounded sure of herself, but I also heard a touch of concern in her voice.

Carlito grabbed a thick binder from the van's center console. He flipped through the plastic filing sheets until he found what he wanted. He pulled out an official-looking yellow document from one of the sheets and exited the van. He said, in Spanish, that he would leave the van running because the starter was acting up.

The four men were heavily armed. One of the men scratched at the collar of his shirt as though he was not comfortable in the clothes. Another gripped his semi-automatic like he was afraid he might drop it.

"I don't like this," I said.

"It's nothing," Lourdes repeated. "They're traffic police."

"They have a lot of guns for traffic police," Alberto said.

Carlito was halfway to the men when the guy with the itchy neck shot him with five, quick bursts. Lourdes screamed. The other three aimed their weapons at the van and fired. Bullets rocked the van, shattered windows. Lourdes bled from her right shoulder. Alberto dove to the floor.

Bullets pounded into the side of the van that faced the shooters. During the barrage I could hear the engine chugging. I jumped to the front and jammed the van into gear. I backed up full speed, turned the wheel with all I had while I stomped on the brakes. The van swayed and tilted but it turned in the opposite direction. The thin tires screeched around the curve. Alberto rolled on the floor and Lourdes fell to my side. She pressed her left hand to her shoulder. Her fingers and blouse were covered in blood.

I pushed the van for all it was worth, but the cop car rapidly gained on us.

"They're going to catch us," Lourdes said. She sounded out of breath, each word passed through gritted teeth.

"Who are they?" I asked, my eyes on the pot-holed asphalt.

"Who knows? They could be Hoochie's men, or Hoochie's enemies."

"Why would he shoot us? We're bringing him the money."

"It's about more than money," she answered.

"What else is there?"

She didn't answer. I glanced at her. Blood flowed freely from the wound in her shoulder. Her eyes were closed. I could see her chest move slightly, so I guessed that she had passed out.

I frantically scanned the countryside as I pushed the van for everything it had. Finally, I saw it: an exit about a hundred yards ahead. The unpaved road disappeared into palm trees and ferns. I figured our chances on the open road were zero to none. Maybe we could lose them in the dense growth. It was all I had as far as ideas.

I waited until the last second, twisted the steering wheel with a grunt and a prayer. The van slid onto the dirt road. We hit rocks and deep ruts, I bounced on my seat like a loose spring. I tried to control the van without slowing it down, but it had taken on its own agenda. It crashed through reeds and grasses. I saw trees, fences and cows rush by. A plume of dust trailed us. It had to be visible for miles. So far, I hadn't seen the cops in the rearview mirror.

I didn't see the ox until we were only a few feet from it. The animal raised its head as we barreled down the road. Its red eyes glared, and its ears stood straight up. I tried the brakes—nothing. I struggled with the steering wheel, but couldn't turn the van. We crashed full-speed into the ox. The animal screamed, the van twisted and crazily turned. I think Alberto hollered something. I saw the roof at my feet. The van crashed to its side and I smashed my head into the driver's door. Something heavy, soft and wet held me there. The last thing I thought as I slipped into unconsciousness was that Lourdes must have landed on me.

# - Chapter 7 -
## THE PINCHE PROBLEM

I woke up in a white room. Walls, chairs, lights—all white. I was even stretched out on a white bed. A tall, black man dressed in red, white and blue stood in the corner. He stared at me for what felt like an eternity, then left the room. I tried to sit up, but my wrists were shackled to the bed. My head ached like the ox had sat on it. A wrap of gauze circled my forehead. My shirt was gone but I still had my pants. A milky haze floated around my brain, disconnecting my thoughts.

A few minutes of silence passed. No windows. Nothing except the bed.

I began to drift off in the whiteness of the room, but I was suddenly assaulted by color. The red-white-and-blue black man returned to the room, followed by a brown woman wearing jeans and a wrinkled blue blazer over a black T-shirt. My eyes and brain finally worked together. I realized the black man was a U.S. Marine in his dress blues.

"Good, you're awake," the brown woman said. "Put this on. Your shirt is a lost cause." She tossed me a gray sweatshirt. "Johnson, take the restraints off. Sorry, Gus, but we weren't sure how you would act when you came to. That was quite a ride, right? And that ox! Where the *fuck* did that come from, right?"

The Marine unlocked the handcuffs and retreated to his corner. I threw the sweatshirt over my head and grunted. A large bruise on my shoulder stung with a sharp pain when I turned my torso. The woman doing the talking stood next to the bed, hands clasped behind her back. She grinned, stupidly, I thought.

"Where am I? What . . . ?"

"You're in the U.S. Embassy clinic. We brought you here from the wreck. You're a lucky man, Gus. We got to you before the Cuban police. That would've been bad."

"Who are you? Where are the people I was with? What . . . " A needle of pain wormed upward through my arm and silenced me.

"Careful, Gus. You're pretty banged up. Just take it easy and I'll explain everything."

I sat back on the bed and waited.

"Eduarda Ventura," she said. "Call me Eddie. Special Assistant to the Consulate. Fancy name for secretary, really. You've been assigned to me, Gus. I'm to take care of you. Make sure you get back home in one piece." She nodded at the Marine. "Eventually," she added.

"What's that mean, you're assigned to me?"

"I'm gonna level with you, Gus."

She was the second person in a few days who assured me they were going to level with me. And yet, I was still lost in the valley.

She cleared her throat. "We know all about your . . . what'll we call it? Job? Contract? Payoff to Hoochie Almeida?"

It wouldn't have done me any good to deny what she said, so I didn't say anything.

"Kino Machaco is a very special person, someone who gets very special attention from people like me. Know what I mean?" Her smile never wavered. "We are quite interested in what he's up to. Him, you must've guessed, his family and friends. So when someone who works for him comes to Cuba with his screwed-up brother . . . well, that gets everyone in a cold sweat, all excited like, here at the Embassy. Know what I mean?" She looked at her Marine and they both smiled. "You were the main topic of conversation these last couple of days. Colorful history. Even a prison stretch."

She winked at me. I thought that was strange.

"We know all about you, Gus."

Perspiration trickled down my ribs. The sweatshirt was too heavy for the warm room. I needed to take it off. I needed water. Food. Sleep. What I didn't need was Eddie Ventura gloating about how she knew everything about me and my mission. I didn't need Eddie, period.

Johnson moved back to my side. He handcuffed me to the bed again, tighter than before.

"However, we must clear a few things up," Eddie said. "You understand that—bottom line, you—individually, are not important, right? Our main concern is national security. Integrity of the U.S. The easiest way to explain it is: we want information from you, you give it to us and you can go home. Or . . . we can send you to my friend, detective Federico Solís of the Havana police, right now. His men are looking for answers to the puzzle of a bullet-ridden taxi van and a slaughtered ox. They'd be pleased as rum punch to learn that an *americano* on an illegal money-exchanging trip to their homeland was involved in the wreck."

She licked her lips, which I personally thought showed a lack of professionalism.

"Killing an ox is very serious. That alone is enough for at least three years in the local prison. Much different from the joint in Colorado where you did time."

My torso twisted in an awkward position because of the handcuffs. I tried to stretch my arms, but it was impossible. My fingers quit tingling and became numb. My shoulder felt like someone had ripped out my rotator cuff.

With clenched teeth I asked, "What are you? CIA? Military? NSA?"

She finally quit smiling. "Nah. Like I said, you ain't that important, Gus. I told you, I'm a simple Special Assistant. But I do have the power to do what I'm telling you. You better believe that."

I hadn't believed most of what she told me, especially that she was a "simple Special Assistant."

"What do you think I know?" I said. "I can tell you what happened out there on the road, but that's not too hard to figure out: the taxi was ambushed by men dressed as police, the driver was killed, one of the passengers was wounded. I tried to escape through the field and I crashed into that damn ox. Now you know everything I know. And, by the way, what happened to the others? Are they okay?"

Eddie strutted to the edge of the bed. She looked down at me with gleaming eyes. She seemed to be enjoying herself—way too much, I thought.

"There's the rub, Gus. That's the whole *pinche* problem, man. The only body we retrieved from the van was yours. No driver, no other passengers. Plenty of blood, including yours, I guess. We know you and Machaco met Lourdes Rivera, and we know none of you were driving when you left the airport. You see, homie, I gotta ask *you:* Where the hell are they?"

She sounded ridiculous. For some reason, she used Chicano slang on me—*pinche,* homie—as if we were *carnales* from the hood, but obviously she wasn't a Chicana. She'd apparently watched too many American movies where *cholos* were the bad guys and they still talked like lowriders from the 1960s. She put her hands behind her back again and leaned to within six inches of my face.

"But more importantly, Gus, and I mean that sincerely, where the hell is the money?"

☙ ☙ ☙

She kept at me for what seemed like hours. Every so often she'd let me have a drink of water, but for most of the time she asked dumb questions and I played dumb with my answers. Her focus stayed on the money, while mine was solely on the others in the van.

I asked why the Embassy would go out on a limb for me, if I was as bad as Eddie insinuated. Why not give me to the Cubans and walk away from the Gus Corral affair? She kind of laughed.

"Politics, amigo," she answered. "Plain and simple. You and the Machaco brothers have the potential to embarrass the U.S., which ain't all that easy these days, considering all the stupid shit that's happened the last couple of years. But there you are, Gus."

"What does that mean?"

"*Mira.* My boss would just as soon avoid the headlines and the urgent red-eye flight to D.C. to explain in person what the hell is going on, know what I mean?"

I nodded.

"So," she continued, "you admit what you were doing. Tell us where the money is, and you're square, maybe just get a warning or some bullshit like that even. Someone higher up on the scale than me talks to Kino, scares the crap out of him, and I can turn in my report. Done and done, brother."

Her irritating smile returned.

"Wish I could help you, Eddie. Tell you what. Give me some food, a few hours of sleep, a flight to Miami and a nice strong drink, and maybe I'll figure out what you're talking about. But, *¿sabes qué?* Right now, at this moment, I don't have a clue."

We danced around like that until she finally called it quits. I'd expected her to forget about asking questions and to turn to rougher methods of persuading me to talk, but other than a few lame slaps in the face, she hadn't touched me by the time she walked out the white door, followed by her black Marine.

I slept, if you can call it sleep when your body is filled with pain, jet lag, hunger and confusion.

# - Chapter 8 -
## ¡EL MARTILLO!

It must have been an hour later when Eddie returned. She marched in the room making as much noise as possible. She'd changed clothes and looked like she'd showered. *She probably ate, too*, I thought. Maybe she talked to her boss. Her sidekick tagged along carrying a red toolbox.

"Wake up, Gus," she shouted. "No more playing around. You're telling me where the money is or it's going to get real ugly in here."

The Marine dropped the toolbox on the floor. He opened it and I could see various pliers, saws, wires and other industrial-looking objects that I supposed were meant to terrorize me into answering questions.

I didn't believe that Eddie had it in her to torture me. She hadn't shown that she was cold-blooded enough to inflict pain. Plus, she was only somebody's assistant, right? A "Special Assistant," to be sure, but still an assistant. How far could she really take this on her own? And why hadn't anybody else talked to me about Kino, the money, Lourdes or Alberto? There had to be more official interest in the incident, even if it was only because a superstar sports celebrity was distantly involved.

But on the other hand I worried that Eddie would take it upon herself to force me to talk as a way of impressing her higher-ups, whoever they were. And knowing Eddie like I did by that time, she would botch the job, and I would pay the price of her incompetence in interrogation.

I went back and forth like this while she stood next to the toolbox, deciding which piece of metal to take out.

"*¡El martillo!*" she shouted.

Johnson grabbed my arm and twisted it against the edge of the bed. He placed his knee in the crook of my elbow and started to push. I had no doubt that he could break my arm, perhaps wreck it permanently if he chose.

My wrists ached from the handcuffs that cut into my skin.

Eddie reached into the box and pulled out a shiny ball-peen hammer. She held it over my arm.

"Does your boss know you're doing this?" I shouted. "You're representing the United States. You sure you want to do this?"

Something wasn't right about the whole scene.

"Talk, motherfucker. Or you leave me no choice. One way or another, you're telling me tonight where that bag of money is stashed. I know you know."

My arm felt like it was already broken. With every word, Johnson leaned more on the elbow. My hands had gone completely numb.

"I'll hit you right in the crease. Your arm will hang limp beside you for the rest of your life. You want that?"

She raised her arm and held the hammer over her head. Her eyes sparkled with the light bouncing off the white surfaces.

"Jesus!" I shouted. "Stop, stop. Okay, okay. I'll show you where the goddamn money is. I'll take you there. Don't hit me with that hammer."

Johnson released his grip on my arm and held up his hand to stop Eddie.

"You're not showing me anything," she said. "Just tell me where it is."

"I buried the bag out there by where we crashed into the ox. I tried to run but I didn't get far. That's when you found me."

"You had time to hide the money?"

"Yeah. There was a hole in the ground, under an old dead palm tree. I threw the money inside and rolled pieces of the palm over it. Then I must have passed out. I can't tell you where exactly, but I know I can find it again. It's all yours. I don't care about the money. I'm only a hired hand without a dog in this fight. You want the money, you can have it. Take me back to where the accident happened, and I'll get the money for you."

Eddie huddled with Johnson in a corner of the room. Johnson was particularly animated, but they whispered so I couldn't hear what they were saying. It sounded like they were speaking Spanish.

Finally, they nodded their heads in agreement.

"Okay, Gus," Eddie said. "Here's the deal. We're going out to the highway. You're gonna get us the money. You pull anything hinky while we're out there and Johnson will shoot you. Understand?"

"Of course," I answered.

She unlocked the handcuffs. Johnson draped a hood over my head, yanked me to my feet and marched me out of the room. I shook my arms and hands to get the blood circulating again.

We turned almost immediately. I waited while they unlocked another door. Then they hustled me down a corridor, I assumed. The temperature cooled dramatically—we had to be under-ground. Eventually, another door opened and it was obvious we were outside. I could feel a warm breeze and smell the ocean. We'd walked into a pleasant Cuban night.

I heard a van's sliding door open, then they tossed me in the back seat. Johnson sat down next to me. I smelled rum and ciga-rettes. Eddie said something from the front. I guessed she was the driver. The van lurched forward and after several minutes it picked up speed. We jerked and bounced over potholes and cracks in the highway, and I knew we were back on the road to the air-port. I thought about what I would do when we stopped at the spot where we'd been attacked, where there was no dead palm tree, no money and no truth to my story.

# - Chapter 9 -
## JUST ANOTHER HOMIE

Other than what flashed past the taxi windows from the airport, I couldn't say I'd seen much of Cuba. My trip so far consisted of a bloody ambush, a collision with an ox who was in the wrong place at the wrong time and hours of a sloppy interrogation by a weird woman who most certainly was not any kind of Embassy assistant. Not exactly what I expected when I agreed to be a bag man for Kino Machaco.

It wasn't rational, but the thing that bothered me the most during that ride in Eddie's van was that, once again, Corrine was right. Jerome, too. There I was, trussed up like a Christmas *tamal* on my way to an appointment with the Cuban woods—a bullet in the back of my head once the truth came out. My body would disappear, most likely tossed into the sea, and one day soon, Corrine and Max and Jerome would gather in the Blind Bat to send up a toast to the mystery of Gus Corral, the private eye who vanished in Cuba the very first day he was on the island.

"Pathetic," Jerome would say.

"Hard-headed," Corrine would add. *"Yo le dije."*

Max would finish the toasts with: "I hope he didn't suffer."

Eddie stopped the van, and Johnson lifted the hood off my face. At first, I saw nothing except the black Cuban night. I was disoriented and lost. Gradually, my eyes adjusted. Stars dotted the sky and a glow on the horizon must have been Havana. We were parked on the road I'd turned onto in my failed attempt to escape. Moon shadows of a jungle of trees, ferns and low bushes surrounded me. My other senses slowly returned. I smelled damp earth, a hint of briny air and the musk of a fermented tropical darkness. I heard the buzz of promiscuous insects and felt careless bugs fly against my face and neck. I stepped on soft dirt that might have been mud. Branches and shrubs swayed in a gentle breeze.

Eddie and Johnson turned on high-power flashlights that lit up the ground at our feet.

"Okay, Gus," Eddie whispered. "You're on, homie. Lead the way."

"Through here, I think."

I trudged along the path the van had made on the gravel road. I whispered only because Eddie had whispered.

"Why you call me homie?" I asked. "You're absolutely not from my hood."

Eddie giggled, Johnson snorted.

"We're both Chicanos, Gus. Chicana in my case." She talked as we walked along the road. "We're from the United States, *ese.* You know what a Chicano is, right? Under different circumstances, we could be in the same crew, hanging out, talking shit."

I almost laughed, but I kept it to myself. I couldn't tell if she was serious, which made her an idiot, or if she was awkwardly trying to keep up her cover, which made her dangerous in a stupid kind of way. Just another homie, my ass.

I stumbled a few times and changed direction more than once, but we made it to where I'd run into the ox. The carnage from the wreck was obvious: smashed trees and bushes, pieces of fly-covered ox carcass and what looked like the front bumper of the taxi.

"It's over there," I said, pointing to a cluster of short palm trees near a rickety wooden fence.

Johnson poked me in the ribs with a pistol I didn't know he had. We moved towards the trees, wary of the rough ground and the rocks loosened by the crash.

I walked as slowly as I could. Eddie led the way.

About ten yards from the cluster, Eddie stopped.

"Shut up," she said, although no one was talking. "What's that? That noise?"

She turned to look over her shoulder, but kept walking. She raised her gun. I stopped. Johnson grunted.

Eddie's silhouette jerked in the moonlight. She tripped on a broken branch and squealed as she fell to the ground. Johnson tensed, but then he was surrounded in light.

Men shouted in Spanish.

"*¡Suelten sus armas!*"

Johnson aimed his gun at the light. A shot exploded, and Johnson tipped over. Eddie got to her knees and aimed her weapon but before she could get off a shot, several men surrounded her, their rifles aimed at her head. She dropped her gun.

I didn't think, didn't wait for something else to happen. I ran into the night, not looking back, expecting a bullet in my back at any second. I twisted and turned with the hope that I could somehow lose the armed men under the cover of darkness. I ran low to the ground, wheezing, out of breath. Sticky blood dripped from the bandage still wrapped around my forehead.

I came to a small rise in the earth. I dashed over it but had to stop suddenly when I saw that I was on the bank of an irrigation ditch and my next step would've landed me in the murky water. I fell backwards and rolled down the hill.

Off to one side, men shouted. Their boots trampled the undergrowth.

I sat up on my knees and waited for the men and their guns.

From somewhere in the Cuban blackness, I heard Lourdes Rivera say, "You are certainly a lot of trouble, Gus Corral. I hope Kino appreciates what I've had to do for you. And I hope you do, too."

☽ ☽ ☽

I passed out. My body had reached its limit: the plane trip from the States, the ambush, the ox, my encounter with Eduarda Ventura and Johnson, not to mention no food and sleep deprivation—all of it was enough to make me roll my eyes into the back of my head and slam my face onto the rich, fertile earth.

When I came to, the sun blazed against a clear, almost white sky. I lay on a hammock strung across the porch of a sprawling, open house. The bright blue-green Caribbean rolled up on a sandy stretch of beach about a hundred yards away. The excited rush of the laughter of children mixed in with the soft sounds of the sea and the urgent calls and whistles of low-flying birds.

I rubbed my hand across my forehead. A small bandage had replaced the gauze. My headache was gone. My arms and fingers felt normal, though bruises ringed my wrists. My stomach growled. Mangoes, bananas, a plastic cup and a pitcher of water sat on a small glass table next to the hammock. I sat up, slowly, eased off the hammock and helped myself to two of the bananas. I was about to start on a mango when Lourdes walked onto the porch from the house.

"Good," she said. "You're awake. You've been out for hours. I hope you feel better."

Her right arm was in a sling.

"What the hell happened?" I asked. "Who killed Carlito? Shot you? That woman and the Marine? Who are they? Where's Alberto? What's going on?"

I was still a bit wobbly and a flash of dizziness made me sit in a wicker chair near the table. I helped myself to a glass of water.

"Yes," she answered. "It's all a mess, isn't it? But maybe I can explain some of it."

Her English carried none of the heavy accents of her brothers.

She looked rested and at ease, quite an accomplishment considering she'd recently been shot and tossed around the inside of a van wreck. Her eyes and the strong jawline reminded me of her brothers, but her skin was lighter than Kino's and her hair not as dark as Alberto's. The little bit I'd dug up on her before I left the States included that she had been a middle manager in the Havana city government, and that she was on friendly terms with many of the most powerful people in Cuba.

She sat down and waited until I finished my water.

First, she talked about Alberto. He injured a leg in the wreck. Nothing broken. He tore a ligament "or something like that," she said. He was in a hospital where doctors watched him and were trying to get his right leg to work again.

"But he's alive," Lourdes said with a hint of relief.

Then she explained that Eduarda Ventura and Johnson were local thugs—"*matones de barrio*"—who were well-known to the Havana police.

"Eddie's not from the States?" I asked. "Johnson's not a Marine?"

"You didn't really buy into their masquerade, did you?"

"Not completely, but they sure worked hard to fool me."

"The so-called Eddie is the wayward daughter of a former administrator in the Bureau of Sanitation Services, a party hack who gave up on her years ago. The man you call Johnson is Mario Faustino, a former farm boy who's nothing but muscle for hire. He's shot up now, in a hospital . . . not where we have Alberto."

I nodded. Finally, something made sense.

"I called an old friend," Lourdes continued. "Inspector Solís of the Havana police. Told him where he could find the two, neatly wrapped and packaged. They're always wanted for something, and I hinted they knew about the dead ox, that maybe they could explain what happened to the poor animal. They won't talk or give up anybody—they've learned that lesson, but they're enough of a menace to themselves that they'll try to outwit the policeman, and so they'll sit in the Havana jail for a few days while Solís makes them sweat."

"He doesn't care that you were involved?"

She sipped her water. "He didn't ask. Federico and I are old friends, from school and even before. I've helped him in the past, and he's watched out for me. He'll let me know if there's something he needs to ask me."

"Who were they working for? They seemed to know a lot about my trip to Cuba and the money."

"I'm not sure. Not for Hoochie, that's certain. He has no reason to steal money destined for him anyway. Maybe they work for themselves. It was a well-known secret among the people that associate with Ventura and Faustino that a large sum of money was coming to the city to be delivered to Hoochie Almeida. Any number of small-time crooks and conmen might try to get to the money before you can give it to Hoochie."

"They ambushed the taxi, shot Carlito?"

She shook her head. "They weren't in on the ambush. They couldn't finance that kind of action, and they don't have the *cojones* for it. They might be involved with the same crew, brought in to get you to give up the money when the ambush didn't give the expected result. They've kidnapped people in the past, so they have some experience that might've helped them."

"You seem to know a lot about these people. What did you say you do for the government?"

She smiled. "I didn't say, but my position is not with internal security or anything like that. I'm a small wheel in a big machine, a lowly bureaucrat. Officially, I'm a supervisor in the Public Information Sector of Havana's Media and Communications Department. That's a fancy name for a person who provides public service data and resource connections to other governmental departments, and to those in the public who might need such information, like farmers, fishermen, tobacco growers. It's not glamorous but I am doing something helpful. At least, I hope so."

I didn't want to be rude, but I couldn't help myself. I slumped in the chair and rubbed my eyes.

"You're tired, and hungry. I'll tell you the rest after you eat and rest some more. Come on in the house. We have food for you."

I followed her into a large room with a massive mahogany table and more wicker chairs. A few plates of fried fish, chicken, black beans, rice and more fruit waited on the table. A bottle of water and a carafe of what I assumed was wine also sat there. The sliding doors that faced the ocean were open. Lourdes must have believed we were safe in the house, even though we'd been ambushed only a day or two before.

A dark older, woman brought warm bread in a basket. Lourdes called her Alma. Lourdes joined me but no one else sat down, although I did hear adult voices and children whispering in the back rooms. A sultry Latin jazz tune played in the background.

I ate more than I should have, and my stomach rumbled like a squall pounding the Malecón. Lourdes took me to a bedroom in the house and said I should sleep, that I probably still had jet lag. I didn't argue.

# - Chapter 10 -
## ISLAND OF SECRETS

When I felt like a human being again—it only took ten more hours of sleep and several plates of rice, beans and plantains—Lourdes finished her explanation.

We sat on a patio under a star-spangled sky. A shimmer of light glowed at the horizon and, although it was late, I didn't think sleep was an option. I drank Havana Club rum mixed with a few drops of Coca-Cola. Lourdes sipped tonic water with a slice of lime. We were alone. The people who'd been in the house when I regained consciousness had left. Lourdes explained they were cousins and the children of cousins.

"Except for Sánchez, the house guard, I live out here alone. He has a small cottage near the beach. He's always close."

As if to convince me, a bearded, stocky man appeared for a second at the edge of the patio. He was older than Lourdes's other men, but he looked as capable as any of them. He slipped into the trees and plants at the back of the house.

"Other men serve as guards at the front gate. Someone's there twenty-four seven. It's the only way to get to the house. We're safe here."

She relayed the details of what happened to us, and then to me. Men who worked for her had followed the taxi from the airport, as a precaution, she said. These men were loyal, many had worked for her husband, Emilio Rivera, when he was alive. Emilio had managed all sorts of enterprises, all legal and state-approved, she assured me, such as a tobacco farm, an art gallery and a taxi service. He had a reputation as an honest man, and the government often used him as an unofficial ambassador in situations that couldn't have an official presence.

"Like what?" I asked.

"Like dealing with the black market. Even the government must accommodate the men, and women, who get their hands on fresh fruit and meat from the countryside, or consumer goods, medicine and tools from places like Mexico and Miami. Sometimes deals must be made. That's the reality of the consequences of the embargo. Emilio was good at that, and he never cheated anyone. Not the black marketers, not the government."

When the ambush happened, her men shot at and frightened off the phony traffic cops, then they followed my crazy driving through the countryside. When they found the wreck, they rushed Lourdes and Alberto into their car and took them to Lourdes' doctor. There was no more room in the car and they left me and my suitcase with one of their men, who hid in the foliage when Eddie and Faustino showed up. He watched as they threw me in the trunk of their car.

Lourdes' man, Virgilio Licona, recognized Eddie and Faustino and guessed they took me to Faustino's market in Havana. As Lourdes explained, the market was usually empty of any goods or food.

"Faustino's no businessman," she said. "And there are the usual shortages of groceries," she added.

Apparently, the "clinic" was an unused meat locker in the basement of the market. Virgilio kept surveillance on the market, and when he saw Eddie, Faustino and I leave, he notified Lourdes. Then she and her men surprised Eddie and Faustino at the accident site.

"But we don't know who set up the ambush, or who Eddie and Faustino were working for," I said.

"I'll find out. This is Cuba. Havana. Everything's a secret, and yet nothing's a secret. People not from Cuba don't understand that. It's complicated."

That was the second time a Cuban wanted me to know that Cuba and Cubans were "complicated."

"But sometime soon," she continued, "I will learn the truth of what happened, and the names of the people who killed Carlito.

In the end, there will be justice for him, and for you, if that's what you want. If you're willing to wait for it."

"Justice is a concept I'm not that familiar with, if you want to know the truth. I was hired for a specific job, and I intend to complete the work. I'm not catching the next flight, but once the money is delivered, and Alberto and Kino are free of this guy Hoochie, I'll be leaving your beautiful island. You can do whatever you think is appropriate to whoever is responsible for the ambush and for Carlito's death. If I'm still here when that happens, and there's any kind of help I can provide, you'll get it. But first things first."

She finished her drink. "In that case, Mr. Corral, I'd better get in touch with Hoochie, so you can finish your job. Leave the rest to me. Unlike you, I know what justice means, and I assure you, there will be justice when this is all over."

The night closed in on us. The breeze gusted and knocked over one of the wicker chairs on the porch. Lourdes stood up and motioned for me to go in the house. We said goodnight.

An hour later I was stretched out on the bed, still awake, still thinking about Lourdes Rivera and her bodyguard and her honest husband who negotiated with the black market. And her promise that justice would be satisfied. I fell asleep as I thought about my upcoming meeting with Hoochie Almeida and the five hundred thousand dollars I was instructed to give him. Somehow that was more comforting than Lourdes' belief that on an island of secrets, there were no secrets.

# - *Chapter II* -
# THE GOLDEN HAVANA NIGHT

Lourdes was gone by the time I crawled out of bed the next day. She'd told me that I couldn't go anywhere, since she hadn't learned who ambushed us on the highway from the airport. The only safe place in all of Havana, apparently, was her house. With nowhere to go, I was forced to loiter on the beach, nap on her patio and listen to a wide variety of Cuban music she'd collected. CDs, cassettes, vinyl. She had it all. The equipment—CD player, record player—was ancient but in good shape, much like the classic American cars from the fifties that rushed through the Havana streets. Old but well-maintained, held together with recycled parts and revolutionary ingenuity.

My only company was Sánchez, the guard. I'd see him about once every hour, patrolling the grounds. He didn't talk, didn't acknowledge my existence, except to pick up empty glasses and plates I left on various tables after I fed myself from Lourdes' well-stocked kitchen.

By mid-afternoon, I decided I had to talk to someone. I had only one option.

"*Oye*, Sánchez," I hollered when I saw the house guard near the backyard wall attacking a tropical bush with a pair of garden shears. "Take a break, man. It's hot. Have a drink with me."

He looked puzzled, so I repeated my request in halting Spanish. That made him grin, the first time I saw any emotion on his face.

"I speak English," he offered. "Takes me a minute, but I understand."

I waved him over. poured him a glass of mango juice from a pitcher on the table and we sat down in the shade.

Gray patches streaked his beard and his hair. His eyebrows were solid black.

"You been with Lourdes long?" I asked.

"With Emilio, first. We were in the army together. Many years ago."

"Did you see combat?"

"Why you ask that?"

"Just curious. I assume the bond between soldiers who've been in battle together is a deep one."

"Cuba hasn't been in a war in decades, before last century."

He sounded angry. I let it go. I didn't bring up the few pieces of military Cuban history that I'd found in my research, like Angola, Bolivia, Che's missions, and more recent allegations of Cuban troops in various hotspots around the world. He didn't want to talk about any of that history. It could all have been capitalist propaganda, and, in truth, I didn't care. I only wanted to start a conversation.

"I'm sorry Lourdes was wounded," I said to change the subject. "I should have been more alert. Those police didn't look right."

"From what she told me, there was nothing you could've done. Those traffic stops are routine, common."

"Carlito, the driver, was killed."

"Anyone who stepped out of the van would have been shot. I'm amazed you made it out of there at all. Lourdes is convinced you saved her life. I am grateful for that."

The more we talked, the more I saw something special in the man. He mentioned a deep affection for Lourdes; his loyalty to her was obvious and strong. They had more than an employer-employee relationship. I was sure of that, but not sure how far it went.

Lourdes returned about seven in the evening. She looked tired, hot. But she didn't rest.

"We're leaving in an hour," she said. "We're meeting Hoochie at his restaurant, El Supremo, in Habana Vieja . . . Old Havana. If the meeting goes well, we'll have a good dinner—it's an excellent restaurant. If it doesn't . . . well, we will have to rely on my men."

"Sánchez?"

"No. He watches the house, that's his only job. My other men will follow us and wait on the street while we're inside. It's the best I can do. Hoochie wouldn't agree to any other place. He was nervous, uptight."

"You already met with him?"

"We had to work out the details of the exchange, and he won't talk about his business or his money on the phone. I don't blame him. Someone's always listening."

"Not the best arrangement," I said.

"No, but we have to deal with it. I'm going to get ready. Have a drink, if you need it."

She headed for her bedroom to get ready.

I poured rum into a blue glass and swallowed a mouthful. If Hoochie was nervous, what did that mean for me?

I walked around the house and looked closely at things I hadn't taken the time to notice.

Lourdes Rivera collected art that wasn't afraid of color. Several nudes hung on the walls. Black and brown women posed on vermillion beds, yellow beaches and against ultraviolet skies. The paintings melted into the subdued blue, brown and orange hues of the house. Slowly fading sunlight bounced off silver and chrome sculptures of mythological animals: minotaurs, dragons and unicorns. The wall that separated the kitchen from the living room was covered with black-and-white photographs of people I presumed were dead relatives. In the center of a shelf was a large framed photo of two bearded young men in military fatigues. They each held an ancient but ominous Kalashnikov. They looked deadly serious. They had to be Sánchez and Lourdes' husband, Emilio.

On another shelf sat more recent color pictures. In one, a boyish-looking Kino Machaco was flanked by young Lourdes Rivera and Alberto Machaco. They smiled broadly, arms around waists. In the background a peeling sign on a whitewashed wall proclaimed *gimnasio de boxeo Rafael Trejo*. Several other young people congregated near the door to the building.

I finished the rum and argued with myself about having a second drink. I reasoned that it might be what I needed to handle the upcoming meeting, but that was bullshit. A second drink of the unfamiliar liquor would make me just high enough to risk crucial mistakes of judgment. Instead, I helped myself to a mango from one of Lourdes' fruit bowls. I sat at a table and waited.

When she emerged, she immediately contacted her men and ordered a car.

"I'll drive," she said. "My men will follow."

She rushed me out of the house. Sánchez stood at the doorway. He wished Lourdes a safe trip. He said nothing to me.

Lourdes drove through rolling countryside on a stretch of narrow paved but rough road until we came to the Havana outskirts. Then she cruised through the twisting and often dark residential streets with barely a nod to other traffic. As she drove, she told me what to expect.

"We'll be seated at a table, we may even order dinner. Hoochie will be watching us and my men outside. He'll want to make sure he knows how many of us there are and whether anyone else is involved, like police or whoever tried to steal the money. When he's satisfied, the waiter will tell us to follow him. I assume we'll go upstairs to his office. That's one place he feels safe. You'll give him the money and say what you have to say on Kino's behalf. I hope you're ready."

"I'm ready," I said with forced attitude. "But I don't have a gun."

"I do," she said. "You don't need one, shouldn't have one. If there's trouble, stay out of the way of my men. If *you're* caught with a gun in Cuba—an American citizen? There's nothing I can do for you. Trust me."

By then we were in the heart of the city, on narrow streets packed with people, cherry-red 1955 Chevrolets and carts, some with horses. The Havana night shimmered with a golden sheen from street lights, the late-setting sun and reflections off cobbled paths and boarded-up shops. Off to our right was a turquoise-colored building that housed a museum dedicated to the Revolution. I could still see broad patches of blue sky smeared with purple clouds. None of it seemed real.

Lourdes parked in front of a well-lit doorway where a man in a white *guayabera* and black pants waited at the top of three small stairs. She jumped out and I followed. I breathed in the smell of Havana and tasted black, sweet coffee, cigar smoke and fried fish. One of Lourdes' men drove the car away. Another handed her a shiny, dark brown leather satchel with a lock across the handles. The doorman signaled for us to follow him inside.

The restaurant décor tried hard to capture a time when gold filigree and enormous red curtains passed for European fashion. Antique chests, chairs and tables gathered dust in enormous dining rooms. Completely out of sync, I thought of the Spanish colonial exhibit at the Denver Art Museum. A few customers sat at a trio of heavy wood tables with benches, but it was still early for Cuban dinnertime. The doorman led us to a small table near stairs that twisted up into a balcony that hung over the kitchen, exposed to viewing by hungry customers.

An open bottle of red wine sat on the table. I poured a glass for Lourdes and one for me. She ignored it. I sipped the wine and regretted it immediately. Wine was not the drink of choice in the neighborhood where I'd first encountered alcohol. I thought about ordering rum but remembered the argument I'd had with myself back at the beach house.

Lourdes hugged the satchel sitting on her lap. She had no trouble carrying it. I figured it was filled with large denominations, hundred dollar bills most likely.

We sat in silence for fifteen minutes. The longer I had to think about what I was doing, the more I realized that I should have listened to Corrine. Lourdes and I were sitting ducks. The men outside could never be fast enough to prevent either one of us from being shot, if that's what Hoochie wanted. My one consolation was that we were delivering money to him, so he had no reason to kill us. But what would happen after we transferred the cash? What was the compelling reason he would allow Lourdes and me to walk out of El Supremo? When he had his money, we'd lose our leverage. I drank more wine even though my throat was tight, and I wasn't sure I could swallow. No one talked to us or asked if we wanted anything. I guessed that the wine marked the limits of Hoochie's generosity.

Miguel Almeida appeared on the stairway. He was dressed in all black: suit, shirt, tie. It was a calculated look meant for Lourdes and me.

"Hola, Lourdes," he said, waving for her to come to him.

We both stood up. I let out a deep sigh. I'd been unaware that I was holding my breath.

The doorman approached and signaled that he was going to search us.

"Miguel?" Lourdes said.

"It's okay, Santos," Hoochie said. "They can come up."

The doorman backed away.

I picked up the satchel—it must've weighed about five or six pounds—and climbed the stairs with Lourdes in front of me. We walked through a short hallway to a pair of doors that opened into a small but comfortable office. The chairs, desk and couch were made of dark wood and leather, but my eyes didn't care about the furnishings. I couldn't look away from the woman who sat on the couch.

"Lourdes, you remember Marí, no?" Hoochie said.

Lourdes stopped. "Marita Valdés. What are you doing here?"

I recognized the woman's face from the photograph at Lourdes' house. A much younger version of Marita stood in the background, off to the side, her eyes focused on Kino.

Lourdes and Hoochie spoke in Cuban Spanish, faster than what I was used to from the *pochos* back home, but I kept up the best I could.

"She's my partner, in all things," Hoochie said. "I thought you knew. She has an interest in our business."

"It was supposed to be just you and me and Gus. You never said anything about her."

The woman stood up. I smelled lilacs. Her black shoulder length hair swayed with her body movement. She wore a red and black outfit that did nothing to hide the fact that she spent a lot of time staying in shape. Her eyes looked like smoke from a dying candle.

"I'll leave if it's a problem, Lourdes," the woman said. "But it's not like we don't know each other."

"She stays," Hoochie said. "Let's just get this over with. Give me the money."

Marita sat down. Lourdes moved closer to me.

"I'll give you the money," I said in English. "But you must understand this is the end of you taking any more bets from Alberto, and of threatening the Machaco family. Do you get that, Hoochie?"

He jerked his head when he heard me use his nickname.

"You insolent pig," he answered, also in English. "I could have you taken out of here, and no one would ever see you again. That is what I understand, you punk. You're nothing but a delivery boy, and the only reason you are here is because the Machaco brothers, as usual, are cowards, afraid to take care of their own dirty business."

Lourdes vehemently shook her head. "You know Alberto's in a hospital, where your men put him, and Kino can't return to Cuba. There's no way they can be here."

"My men have done nothing to Alberto. You're talking nonsense. Your brothers have always found excuses for avoiding their responsibility, for standing up to their mistakes, like when Joaquín killed Claudio."

"Don't start with that, Miguel. Leave that in the past where it belongs. We're here to pay off Alberto's debt. The money's yours. Just stay away from Alberto. That's all."

Hoochie slapped his thigh. A high-pitched laugh slipped through his lips. "You have always been naïve, Lourdes. Nothing's changed about you. Give me the damn money and get out. You have two minutes, that's all you're getting from me."

"Then I guess the bag stays with me," I said.

He reached for the bag and I pulled back. His face tightened, and his eyes flared. He tried to grab me, but I moved away, and he tripped on his feet. He regained his balance before he fell. His hand gripped a small revolver. He started to scream profanities, when the door to the office opened.

"What is it?" Hoochie hollered. "I said no one was to bother us!"

I turned and saw Santos, the man in the *guayabera,* pull a gun from the back of his pants. He aimed in our direction.

I jumped to Lourdes and knocked her to the floor. The gun exploded. The satchel flew from my hands.

I heard another shot that I thought must have come from Hoochie.

Marita screamed. Hoochie fell backwards against his desk, blood streaming from his neck.

A bright circle of blood stained the gunman's *guayabera.* He reached down and picked up the bag of money, then he dashed back through the door and raced down the stairs. I heard shouts and thuds, and then a series of gunshots.

Before I could get to my feet, several armed men rushed into the office.

# - Chapter 12 -
## CENTER OF ATTENTION

Inspector Federico Solís of the National Revolutionary Police Force paraded through the remains of El Supremo like a hyper-feral cat. He rushed around the restaurant, barked orders and appeared to examine every bullet hole, broken piece of glass and blood splatter. He was a short man, maybe five-six, with a potbelly that bulged from within his drab, gray jacket. He was thin, brown and had gray, wiry hair that sprang from his head and ear lobes. The beat cops on the scene jumped at his words and were submissive to the point of embarrassing themselves.

I sat with Lourdes at a table on the first floor. Solís stopped his scurrying when he saw her, shook his head and then proceeded up the stairs, where Hoochie's body remained, drained of much of its blood.

Santos died on the stairs. Hoochie had wounded the shooter, and then his men finished the job. The gunman fell to the first floor and his body lay near the table where Lourdes and I had originally sat, before the meeting. The police covered the dead gunman with a tablecloth. Everyone avoided the body; a few of the cops averted their eyes if they came close to it.

One of the uniformed cops, a young guy with a trace of a mustache and very shiny boots, held the satchel with both of his hands. He leaned against a wall, not talking to anyone, not doing anything except keeping his stranglehold on the money.

Marita Valdés stayed upstairs with Hoochie. She cried out about every five minutes. When I asked Lourdes what that was about, Lourdes shook her head.

"Nothing that makes sense," she said. "Marita's hysterical. They'll probably take her to a hospital."

I learned through my research on Cuba that although there was crime on the island, most of it was low-level or non-violent and usually related to simple survival: the black market, bribery of officials who could make life a bit easier, theft of clothing, gasoline, bread. Hoochie's lucrative criminal enterprise was unusual. I figured that he must've paid off the right people, for a long time, to keep operating for so many years as a bookie and general racketeer. The shoot-out in his restaurant also was unusual, something that just *did not happen* in Havana. There were murders, of course, but those normally were crimes of passion or desperation, not hit-jobs on well-known, important men in very public places. Hoochie had died as he lived: the center of attention, against all the rules.

"Hoochie's finally dead," Lourdes said.

We each had a glass of water that one of the policemen had given us on Solís' order. If I had been someone, maybe anyone else, we may have raised them and drank out of solemn respect. But even in the dead man's own restaurant we let the moment pass. She looked like she wanted to talk, so I encouraged her.

"Good or bad?" I asked.

"For years I've prayed that he would die, and now it's happened. It's good for Alberto, of course. And now Kino can stop worrying about what Hoochie might do. And it's good for Cuba. We don't need men like him. We have too many as it is."

"How about for you? This must be good for you, too. Maybe your life can get back to normal."

Her laugh stopped almost as quickly as it started. "What is normal?"

Solís appeared at the top of the stairs. He was several feet from us, but I could see the restaurant lights reflecting off his sweaty forehead. He pointed at Lourdes and gestured for her to go to the young cop holding the satchel. Solís walked down the stairs and waited for her.

Lourdes and the detective huddled with the young cop. They talked for a few minutes. Solís became more animated the longer the conversation lasted until, finally, the young cop transferred the satchel to him. Solís handed it to Lourdes. The younger cop walked away.

Lourdes reached into the satchel and took out a thin package of what I guessed was one-hundred-dollar bills, probably a thousand dollars' worth. Solís grabbed the package and made his way back up the stairs.

The restaurant had turned hot and stuffy, heavy with the smell of blood and gunshots and death. About a dozen plainclothesmen and uniformed police were on the scene, many smoking cigarettes. Another dozen or so restaurant workers stood nervously in the kitchen, obviously worried about their jobs and the possibility of a visit to the Havana jail. The gunman's shrouded corpse remained on the floor. A pool of blood surrounded the upper body, and blood splatter marked the stairs and portions of the wall. My forehead felt warm and clammy.

"We can leave," Lourdes said. "Solís knows what happened. He will find out who the shooter was and who he works for. Then, maybe, this will end. And things, as you say, can get back to normal."

We were about to walk out the door, when Solís appeared again at the top of the stairs.

"Lourdes!" he shouted. "I just got a call. Your man at the house—he's been killed. Your house was attacked. There's been a fire. You can't go back there."

I caught most of what he said but I had to be sure.

"Sánchez is dead?"

She nodded, then her body wobbled. She leaned into me and I held her up. Her head fell onto my chest, where she buried her muffled sobs.

๑)) ๑)) ๑))

Solís offered to take us in for the night. The beach house had been saved from the fire, but no one could stay there. And Solís also didn't think Lourdes should stay in the apartment she kept in the city.

"Havana's not safe for you," he said to Lourdes.

He'd learned that Sánchez's throat had been cut. The man had bled to death with a rifle in his hands. There were no other bodies. Lourdes took the news hard. Esteban Sánchez had worked for her for twenty years.

"He was a gentle man, a poet," she said. "He studied flowers and plants and played the piano. They didn't have to kill him."

She wanted to leave the city as soon as possible. She made a few phone calls from the restaurant, and then one of her men drove us to Solís' place. The detective told her not to travel in her own car. Solís said he would join us later, when he completed what had to be done to officially process the shooting.

Inspector Solís' house looked unfinished. The front door was at the back of a row of concrete buildings that I thought were small warehouses or storage units until I realized they were homes. The area did not have street lights, and the golden aura of Havana did not reach into the dark alley where one of the city's top cops lived. Some of the buildings had broken windows. Dim light shined through cracks and loose door jambs. The sidewalk was nothing more than cracked bricks and boards strewn along a muddy path.

Solís had given Lourdes a key, and she let us in. She made a pot of strong coffee and turned on a flickering television set that broadcast music and dance videos. She poured two cups and dropped several cubes of sugar into each one.

Wooden chairs crowded the kitchen. Peeling cupboards held chipped plates, cracked glasses, stained cups. A wall clock had a painting of Che Guevara on its face.

"Federico got that from a relative in Miami," Lourdes explained. She had not spoken on the trip from the restaurant.

Next to the clock a framed yellowing certificate declared a celebration to honor the "exemplary courage and devotion to duty" of the "much respected" Inspector Federico Solís.

"You must want an explanation," Lourdes said when we sat down in the shabby kitchen.

"That'd be good."

"I should begin with the inspector."

"Okay. Good start."

"Federico earns about thirty dollars a month. That's the going rate for teachers and doctors, too, so he's doing good, if he has another job, which he does at times. This place is what he can afford. Most of Havana lives like this. Everyone has a home, or so we are told. Some have better homes."

I didn't think the irony was lost on her.

"You gave him money. You bribed him?"

She sipped the coffee and shook her head. "It's not like that. That money is to pay him for his services, and to share with his men. It's the way the system works, the only way it works. Like I said, police don't make much money—very few Cubans do, so we have other ways of providing. Federico's a decent policeman, mostly honest. The money I gave him won't change that. He will find out who killed Hoochie and he will arrest him." She paused. "Unless he gets other orders. That can happen if there are more important things going on than the simple assassination of a loan shark and criminal. I told you before: living in Cuba is complicated."

"I'm starting to believe you."

I tried the coffee. The rich sweet liquid coated my throat and then my stomach. It was probably my imagination, but I felt instantly awake and alert, something I hadn't experienced since before I landed at the Havana airport.

"What if he thinks you were involved, or me?"

"Then he will arrest you, or me." She set down her empty cup. "But we don't have to worry about that, do we?"

"I know I didn't have Hoochie killed."

"But you wonder about me? Really?"

I shrugged. "There's something going on that I don't understand completely, maybe that I'll never understand. It's *complicated.*"

She smiled.

"But here we are," I said. "Now what?"

I drained my cup, sat back in my chair and waited for Lourdes to tell me our next steps. I briefly thought that perhaps I could go home now. I'd tried to do what I'd been hired to do. The killing of Hoochie was not part of the plan, but wasn't I finished with Cuba? I answered my own question by shaking my head. My job wasn't just about delivering the money, it never had been. Kino Machaco wanted the threat to his family removed, neutralized. That's what I'd been paid for, with more money waiting for me if and when I did return to Denver, but only if the work was well and truly finished. Lourdes was running for her life, hiding in a back street, plotting an escape from someone who'd already killed her driver, house guard and her brothers' tormentor. Clearly, the threat still existed, only in a form different from Hoochie.

The rickety front door opened. Inspector Solís and Marita Valdés walked in. The cop looked even more wrinkled and tired. Marita's dress was blood-stained. Make-up smeared her face.

"Marita," Lourdes said. "Why am I not surprised?"

It wasn't really a question.

# - Chapter 13 -
## BAD FOR BUSINESS

The Cuban cop fiddled around his tiny, decrepit home like a bad Columbo impersonation. He obviously grasped that tension existed between Lourdes and Marita. Hell, even I could feel it in the dank atmosphere of the worn-out kitchen. He chose to ignore it. He made more coffee and poured everyone a cup. He brought out a platter of stale cookies, a small baguette and a jar of very red jam.

We sat at the table. The blinking TV played in the background, but I couldn't hear anything specific.

He introduced me to Marita. I doubted she'd heard him.

"You should leave as soon as possible, Lourdes," Solís said after finishing a small chunk of bread and jam.

"That's my intention," Lourdes answered. "What is *she* doing here?" She nodded her head at Marita.

"I'm afraid, Lourdes," Marita said before the cop could answer. "Surely you appreciate that. Federico thought it might be safer for both of us if we worked together."

Solís nodded.

"Miguel . . . " Marita's voice trailed off.

"I can't work with you. You and Hoochie have . . . there's no way I can forget our past, your lies and deceit."

"That wasn't me," Marita said.

"You or Hoochie . . . what's the difference? This all happened because of Hoochie and his abuse of my brothers. He has only himself to blame for his own death. He deserves..."

Marita sprung from her chair. Her coffee tipped over and spread in a dark circle.

"Don't . . . you can't . . . " She reached across the table for Lourdes.

Solís grabbed her and held her back. "Marí, Marí! Calm down. Lourdes!"

He pulled Marita out of the kitchen and disappeared into a dark room separated from the kitchen with a bamboo curtain. Lourdes found a rag and cleaned up the coffee. Marita's moans filtered into the kitchen. Solís whispered. Drawers opened and then were shut.

Solís returned a few minutes later. "I gave her something to sleep," he said. "Half of my job is calming down witnesses, victims."

"She's no victim," Lourdes spit out.

"You have to listen to me," Solís said. "She's in bad shape. She's afraid for her life. Someone is after you, and it appears that same someone had Hoochie killed. The burning of your home and the shooting . . . it's too much of a coincidence. Marita could easily also be a target."

Lourdes stared at her policeman friend but didn't say anything.

"What are you thinking?" I asked.

"I know this will be difficult," Solís answered. "But it makes sense to me."

Lourdes stiffened against her chair.

"You leave Havana, tonight or early tomorrow. I have family in Trinidad. They manage a hotel . . . well, it's an old mansion that was built by one of Batista's cousins. It's not the Hilton but it's safe. You can stay there."

"And Marita?" I asked.

"She can't handle this alone. Together, you three can wait this out until I track down the person responsible for the attacks on you and Lourdes, and Hoochie's murder. Both of your families have enemies. Apparently, some are the same."

"You're insane," Lourdes responded, her words heavy with anger. "I can't do that. You know what that woman has put me through. You know our history. I don't care what happens to her. I don't care."

"When did Marita become Lourdes' problem?" I asked. "I can go with Lourdes wherever she thinks it's safe. But this Marita should fend for herself. I don't see any other way."

Solís shook his head. "Lourdes can answer that better than me."

Lourdes stood up and put her cup in the rusty sink. She talked with her back to the cop and me. "Federico thinks I have an obligation to Marita. Never mind all the trouble and problems she's caused my family over the years. He thinks I have a debt to her. I guess he's saying this is the time to pay it off."

"What could you owe her for?" I asked.

A gust of wind smashed against the house. Rattles and squeaks erupted, and for a second I worried that a tropical storm might rip out Solís' home from its cracked foundation.

Lourdes turned and faced us. "For one, Marita's family helped Kino when he left Cuba. That's what he's talking about."

"It was more than simple help," Solís said. "Her family was close to the government. It goes back to the Revolution. The men in that family fought with Che and Fidel. Marita's great-grandfather died in one of Batista's prisons. Her father worked under Raúl Castro for years. Without the help of the Valdés family, Joaquín Machaco would not be playing baseball in the United States."

"That wasn't Marita," Lourdes insisted. "She had nothing to do with Kino's escape."

"You know that is not important, Lourdes. It was her family. The Valdés people took a big risk for *your* family. Now, a Valdés needs your help. It's only right that you do what you can."

"Not if it means setting herself up as a target," I said.

Solís looked at me as though I'd grown a tail or lost an eyeball.

Before he could respond, Lourdes interrupted. "Federico! Please. I'm in hiding, running from people I don't know, for reasons I don't know. I can't help myself . . . so what can I do for her?"

"You can take her with you, keep her safe until I finish my job and bring in the killer. You can watch her, protect her if necessary. Depending on where you go, I can have someone with you."

"I'll be with her," I said. "I'm still working for her and the Machaco brothers."

"And what? Does that make me feel more secure about Lourdes' safety?" He answered his own question. "No, not in the least."

Lourdes clutched the cop's hands. "Gus saved my life, Federico. Twice. He drove us out of the ambush, and he knocked me down when the shooting started in El Supremo. He could have been shot himself. Both times. I trust this man."

The cop grumbled to himself. He slouched into his ill-fitting jacket. His face wrinkled as though he had a very bad case of heartburn.

"There are other reasons you should help Marí. You've not forgotten that, I hope."

Lourdes shrugged. She said nothing about the "other reasons" that Solís mentioned.

"Why are you so invested in what happens to Lourdes and Marita?" I asked. "What's in it for you?"

Solís straightened up. "Mr. Corral? Gus? Correct?"

Lourdes and I both nodded.

"You might not understand. Cuba is at an historic juncture: the death of Fidel, the change in, uh, perspective by the government, the loosening of travel restrictions and the trade embargo by the U.S., if only for a short period. Cuba is changing, growing. This thing that happened tonight . . . well, it's bad for business. I'm a public servant. I work for the common good. I take that responsibility very seriously. I've been instructed to put everything else aside and to concentrate on this series of events that began when you arrived in Cuba. Which means I focus on the people most directly involved in those events. Lourdes. Marita. And you, Mr. Corral."

I didn't like the emphasis he put on me. He smiled, awkwardly, as if his face was not comfortable with high levels of expression.

"You want us together," I said. "The better to keep an eye on us?"

"Something like that."

"I'm leaving Havana," Lourdes said. "We won't be around. What about Alberto?"

"I have men watching him, twenty-four hours a day. He's safe. If he's released from the hospital, I'll send him to you."

She nodded. "I'll stay away forever if I have to."

"You won't need to do that," Solís assured her. "Take Marí with you. Give me a few days, and Havana will once again be safe for you. I have resources available. You are important, respected by many people in the government. I will be given all the help I need. And the government wants the violence stopped quickly. If I can't do that, then others will take over. You know that won't be good, Lourdes . . . for any of us."

She nodded again, reluctantly.

We talked for several more minutes. Eventually, we agreed that Lourdes and I would leave Havana in the morning for Trinidad, a village to the southeast, where Solís believed she would be safe. Marita Valdés would travel with us. When Solís sent word, we'd return to Havana and then, I hoped, I could finally go home to Denver.

Solís found blankets for us and tried to create beds out of chairs and pillows. He climbed a ladder and stretched out on the floor of a miniature loft that hung over the kitchen. Lourdes slept in the only comfortable chair in the place, an oversized recliner that looked as old as the house. I crashed on the floor and I got very little sleep.

Too many questions picked at my brain. Why was Solís so insistent that Marita travel with us? Why was he so sure he could end the crime spree in a few days? Who "instructed" him to prioritize Hoochie's murder, to the exclusion of everything else? I had several concerns about the Havana detective. But they were nothing compared to my anxiety about Lourdes. I knew very little about her. Sister of a Cuban defector making millions playing baseball in the major leagues. She was obviously well off, by Cuban or North American standards. She was given deference and space by police and, it appeared, government officials. How had she accumulated her wealth and her status? Why did she have men "working for her"? Why had someone attacked her house and killed her house guard on the same night that someone killed the enemy of her brothers? The more I thought about my situation, the more questions popped into my head, and the more answers I didn't know.

The night turned into a crazy montage of images and disconnected conclusions: dead men sprawled on restaurant floors, blood-splattered walls, screaming oxen, beautiful Cuban women dancing on new graves. Deep into my morbid insomnia, I heard a gentle patter of rain against the grimy windows. It pulled me back from the nightmare and I started to doze off almost peacefully.

A massive flash lit up the room, and I saw Lourdes in that instant. Her eyes were open, staring at me. The crash of thunder shook the cups in the sink and the few pictures on the wall. Lourdes said something I couldn't make out, then silence. I held my breath and waited.

I felt as if the night had stopped, as if the darkness had taken root. No sounds came from outside, and the only thing I heard in the house was the steady tick-tock of Solís' Che clock.

A few seconds passed.

A heavy, monotonous drumbeat pounded the house. I breathed again. The storm lasted until the first gray rays of morning slipped through the makeshift curtains.

# Part Two

# - Chapter 14 -
## ROCKIN' WITH RITCHIE

Trinidad is about three hundred and fifteen kilometers from Havana. To get us there, Lourdes secured another yellow taxi van with a driver, a short, pudgy guy who called himself Juanito.

We'd wanted to leave early, around seven, but we were delayed until almost ten. Solís provided a breakfast, but he was a slow cook. He measured everything, more than once, and his stove wouldn't cooperate. He left the house twice for things he didn't have.

Then we waited for Lourdes' men to bring her a change of clothes and other necessities she would need in Trinidad.

The biggest wait was for our driver, who showed up with a hangover. He explained that the only message he'd received was that he had to pick us up before noon, so he thought he was doing well.

When we finally took off from Solís' hovel, Marita sat in front with Juanito, Lourdes stretched out in the back and I had the middle seat.

The ride from Havana was long and exhausting, but quiet, uneventful, a surprise to all of us. I finally saw Cuba the country instead of Cuba the crime scene. Groups of students dressed in school uniforms lined sections of the highway, waiting for buses. Hitchhikers were waved off by Juanito with a cupped hand signal, which I learned meant that his taxi was full. Horse- and ox-drawn carts competed for space on the highway shoulder with massive billboards that urged the people to "NEVER FORGET THE REVOLUTION". Small villages would appear suddenly along the way, populated with free-roaming chickens, farmers leading goats and dogs, and laughing women sitting in the glassless windows of thatched shacks and unpainted cement buildings. About every five miles, fruit and vegetable vendors hovered around less-than-full tables of produce. An occasional hand-painted sign announced a restaurant inside one of the houses. Traffic was thin but consistent: generally noisy, smoky trucks, taxis in various shapes and colors, and the periodic, packed tour bus that sped past us as though we were parked.

Juanito listened to music through a set of earphones that he hooked up to an antique pocket tape recorder.

Marita Valdés looked tired, washed-out, but still beautiful. If I hadn't known better, I might've described her as a melancholy angel. She wore a sweatshirt she'd borrowed from Solís, jeans and boots. No make-up. She looked straight ahead, not talking, not really moving.

Lourdes fell asleep and about an hour into the drive we all heard her snoring. Marita turned and looked toward the back of the van. Her eyes moved to me, she smiled. I couldn't help myself, I smiled back at her. I told myself to be cool with the widow.

"You are a long way from home, Mr. Corral," she said in uneasy English.

"Yeah. Cuba is nothing like Denver."

She twisted in her seat to look more directly at me. The van's motor was loud, and the road was rough. We shook and rattled like a covered wagon on the Santa Fe Trail. I wasn't sure I would hear all that she said, so I leaned forward.

"Denver? Where Kino lives? Not a coincidence that you work for Lourdes."

I wasn't sure how much I should tell her. I nodded.

"Tell me, Mr. Corral." She paused, searching for the right words.

I imagined what she would say. I was wrong.

"Did you know my husband was going to be killed last night? Did you have anything to do with his death?"

I lost whatever cool I had left. I shook my head, twice. I tried to come up with a few words that made sense. "We were all targets last night, including Lourdes. That's what I know, señora."

"Yes, I saw your brave act, your saving of Lourdes. Too bad no one could save Miguel."

"You think that somehow Lourdes was involved with the death of your husband?'

"It is not a secret that Lourdes and Miguel were enemies. At least, no secret to me. Their lives have been mixed up for years."

She looked again to the back. Then she turned her bloodshot eyes on me. "You don't know. You couldn't know." Her eyes bored deeper into mine. "They were lovers, once. Not that long ago."

She paused. Her eyes blinked a tear away. "There is no greater hatred than the one that grows from a love destroyed by betrayal or guilt. Lourdes knows that only too well."

"If that's true, it's still no cause for murder."

I wanted to ask more, to dive through the whirlpool at the heart of the history of the Machaco and Almeida families. The love affair, the death of the younger brother, Claudio, the repayment of a debt that had caused more deaths, more pain. But I couldn't do it. Not with Lourdes in the van, not with the grieving widow staring at me with her tragic eyes.

"You're talking like a child," she said. "Love is the perfect cause for murder." She turned to the front and curled up in her seat.

"We have to work together," I said. "The death of your husband hasn't stopped this . . . whatever it is. Your friend, detective Solís, believes we are all in danger. He sent Lourdes and you away from Havana because of that. If we don't watch out for one another, we might not ever get back to Havana."

She didn't respond. I gave up trying to talk to her.

ꙮ ꙮ ꙮ

We traveled slowly, primarily because of the rough condition of the highways. We had to take a detour along an indirect route because of a washed-out bridge, and that cost us another hour. We stopped twice to eat and to use restrooms at tourist rest stops that were clean and attractive and offered souvenir trinkets such as Fidel keychains and books in Spanish about Ernest Hemingway.

Several hours into the drive, Lourdes told Juanito to pull over into one of the parks along the Bahía de Cochinos, the Bay of Pigs. She wanted to stretch her legs. Juanito did as she ordered, and in a few minutes, we sat on a rocky ledge over blue-green water that covered the horizon for as far as I could see. I was familiar with the history of the bay, and I wasn't surprised when Lourdes said that a museum existed up the road in Playa Girón that was devoted to the battle and the defeat of the CIA-sponsored invasion. I told her I'd catch it next trip.

About fifty yards from where we parked, a group of young people gathered around a shack that sold beer and bottled water. Music could be heard from a player of some type on the back wall.

Lourdes and I walked to the stand. Marita stayed with Juanito near the van.

I ordered a Bucanero, Cuban beer. Lourdes asked for papaya juice. The drink stand's workers, two young men and one young woman, played checkers and listened to Yankee rock 'n roll. When the Ritchie Valens' rendition of *La Bamba* started, I heard the young people sing along. I joined them, best as I could anyway. When the song ended, I thought I'd explain why Richard Valenzuela changed his name. They were familiar with Ritchie and his sad story, and it didn't take them long to figure out that I was a *pocho* Chicano who spoke broken Spanish. They knew about Chicanos in the States. They started giving me an "*órale*" for this and an "*ese*" for that and a "*qué pasa, güey*" for something else. They laughed every time one of them said "*güey*."

A 1956 Nassau Blue and India Ivory Chevy Bel Air parked at the stand. From the way the driver was greeted, with cheers and hugs, he had to be a member in good standing of the drink stand's regular crowd. The main bartender pointed at me, then said something about a *mexicano* from *los Estados Unidos.*

The driver, whose name appeared to be Patito, eagerly shook my hand and asked if I'd ever been to Los Angeles. I said, "*Claro*," and then he proceeded to brag about the original equipment on the beautifully maintained car: taillight lenses, hubcaps and a few other small items. The interior looked to be covered in leather, but

Patito shook his head when I asked. He also explained that the engine was from an Isuzu, the transmission from a Peugeot. He asked if I would like to go for a ride.

I turned him down just as Lourdes waved at me to return to the van. The workers exuberantly wished us a good trip. When I shouted, "*Ay te watcho,*" they looked at me like I'd spent ten minutes too long in the Cuban sun. I'd taken the Chicano thing as far as it could go on the road to the Bay of Pigs Museum in Playa Girón.

# - Chapter 15 -
## EL HOTEL FRANCÉS

The drive from Havana lasted ten hours, which seemed like a very long time for three hundred and fifteen kilometers, but Lourdes thanked Juanito for doing a good job, bought him a pineapple and a bunch of plantain as a tip, and no one complained about the time.

The hotel in Trinidad lived up to Solís' description, and then some. At one time, probably in the 1940s, El Hotel Francés must have been elegant. Lourdes told me it had been the home for Batista relatives. It was a high-ceilinged mansion with intricate iron work, frescoed angels and small rooms that barely held a bed. The huge square-shaped building featured an open, sunken courtyard in the middle of the square. The cracked steps to the courtyard were covered with potted ferns and tongue-flicking lizards. Vines and agave plants snaked up the stained walls.

The three of us—Lourdes, Marita and me—were the only guests. After Juanito unloaded us, he drove the van away without a second glance. Lourdes said he would stay with relatives. We met the owner, Margarita Durand, found our rooms and cleaned up.

We sat down with Margarita, Solís' cousin, for coffee in a cluttered room with a long table and a bed. Huge, purple drapes hung on barred windows that stretched from the floor to the ceiling. Margarita said the bedroom was her office.

She had long, gray hair and dressed only in silk pajamas: torn, faded and thin, but silk, nevertheless. Pale, glassy skin stretched over a reedy frame and gray eyes folded in on themselves. Margarita loved to talk and before an hour had passed I learned, among many other things, that Margarita's mother, Constancia, suffered from dementia, that the elderly woman roamed the hotel at any hour of the day or night, looking for Jacques, her long-dead husband, an émigré from France. She said, we should avoid the marketplace nearest the hotel and do business only with the artists around the town square. She also said that although she called herself the owner, *la dueña*, ninety percent of what the hotel earned went to the government, "like any common tobacco farmer or *éleveur de chèvre.*" We stared blankly. "Goatherder," she explained.

Eventually, Margarita led us to the dining area where she fixed a light dinner of chicken soup and mango salad. The room faced the courtyard, and I felt as though we were more outside, in the courtyard, than in the hotel. The place had the feel of space and airiness, and the town's smells and sounds floated down to us.

Margarita chatted while preparing the meal and didn't stop when she served us. Lourdes added a little to the conversation, but most of the time we listened to our host's tales of government corruption, which robbed her of a "basic standard of living," or, in contrast, government heroes who stayed at the hotel since the Revolution. She spoke fondly of Che, Camilo, Barbaroja and Aleida, but she left the impression that she was not a fan of Fidel.

Occasionally, I saw an elderly bent woman mumbling to herself as she glided by in the background. That's when I realized the full implication of the fact that I was on my own. I didn't know these people, not really. I worked for Lourdes, and I'd been given a form of the third degree and almost killed because of my relationship to her, but I didn't know any details about her. I knew less, a lot less, about Marita, Margarita and the ghostly presence that roamed the dark hallways of the hotel.

I'd lost my cell phone days before, along the way, maybe when I rammed the ox, but service was limited anyway, so it didn't really make a difference. I needed to talk with Jerome or Corrine, or Kino Machaco. But I had no way to contact them—no easy way that wouldn't attract the attention of local police or anyone who might be looking for us.

There I was, a lone Chicano detective in Cuba, bumping up against old feuds and older secrets, not sure what to do for my next move. The feeling was familiar. Except for my location, I could have said, "Same old, same old."

# - Chapter 16 -
## THE WORM AND THE PATRIOT

When we finished eating, Marita excused herself and shuffled to her room. Lourdes and I stayed with Margarita. We drank wine and coffee while we listened to her stories of the famous and infamous guests she'd entertained at the very same table where we sat. Margarita offered me a cigar, which I declined. She insisted that I take it anyway. I stuck it in my shirt pocket. The mother flitted by a few times, and I heard her curse in Spanish and French and ask an unseen listener if he enjoyed the stew.

Shadows slowly crept into the hotel along the pale-yellow courtyard walls. Brown ferns and sparse vines drooped from thirst. The lizards clung to the ground, unable to move, or not wanting to. Margarita's face was half in darkness, half in light from an early moon. Her skin looked thin, parched. Lourdes stared with black-ringed eyes. I was surrounded by decay and stagnation.

Margarita turned on a few dim lamps and, again, the Cuban night washed over us with soft, golden light.

Rhythmic dance music filtered into the hotel from jamming musicians on the steps near the square. The ever present noisy trucks lumbered through the streets with squeaky brakes and rough gears, and I thought I heard the growl of a wild animal.

The feeling of solitude wouldn't leave. The mix of wine and coffee fueled my inherent paranoia. I worried about Lourdes and the money. I even worried about Marita and her grief. I imagined gunmen storming through the massive wooden doors of the hotel, or an intruder prowling our rooms, waiting. But at the heart of my worry were thoughts of what else might happen to me, what else could happen to me? And I struggled against the idea that I might never get off the island of Cuba.

§» §» §»

Alberto Machaco showed up around midnight. He traveled with Lourdes' man, Virgilio Licona, who wore a conspicuous shoulder holster under his jacket. The two men stumbled into the hotel, red-eyed, hungry and jittery.

Licona said only a few words. He answered Lourdes' questions about the trip and confirmed that no one had followed them from the hospital. He mentioned that Solís had arrested the woman I knew as "Eddie," Eduarda Ventura, but that's all he knew about the small-time thief. His voice was rough, and he smoked constantly. He excused himself to the courtyard when he lit a cigarette, so he was often away from the group.

Alberto looked especially bad. The cool, confident man I'd met in the Los Angeles airport now appeared lost, unsure. He walked on crutches; a metal brace supported his right leg. He appeared to be in intense pain.

"You sure you should be out of the hospital?" I asked after everyone found a chair and held a drink.

Margarita warmed the soup and served two bowls to the men.

"No choice." His subdued voice almost disappeared in the late-night sounds of the town.

"Solís said he couldn't guarantee my safety. His men are chasing down every lead on who the shooter at the restaurant was working for. The killing is a huge embarrassment for the government. Solís talked about how it was bad for business."

"He told us the same," I said. "He must be getting a lot of heat."

"I don't trust that man," Virgilio said.

It was the first time I'd heard him speak without being asked a direct question.

"You mean Solís?" I asked. "Why?"

"Because Federico's a policeman," Lourdes said quickly. "Virgilio has his prejudices."

"Call it what you want." His raspy words were difficult for me to understand. "I feel better for you, Lourdes, that you're away from Havana and out of the reach of Solís."

"I don't care about all that," Alberto said. "What's next? I only want to leave this damn island and return to my home."

His words echoed my thoughts and they visibly upset Virgilio, Margarita and Lourdes.

"You call that country your home, after all the suffering the U.S. has caused for your people, for us?" Lourdes said.

"I owe nothing to Cuba or the so-called Revolution," Alberto answered, with more force than I thought he could dredge up. "Any suffering is either the fault of Castro and his criminal government, or you yourselves for letting the communists control your lives."

Virgilio grabbed Alberto's sleeve. I jumped to my feet— Alberto was part of my job, too.

Before I said or did anything else, Lourdes tapped Virgilio's shoulder and he released his grip on Alberto. He walked towards the courtyard, pulled a cigarette from a wrinkled pack, but then put it away and returned to us.

I sat down.

"You island Cubans amaze me," Alberto continued. "You complain about the lives you are forced to live, and yet, you forget why that is so, and you are willing to die for that man and his so-called Revolution."

"Yes, Alberto," Lourdes said. "We still love our country. We still believe in our country"

"And the Revolution," Virgilio added. "No matter what you *gusanos* say."

Alberto raised his palms as a sign of peace. "We won't settle our disagreement tonight. It's an old conversation. I shouldn't have said anything and I apologize."

Lourdes and Virgilio nodded their agreement.

"The money? It's safe?" Alberto asked.

"Yes," Lourdes answered. "As safe as we are."

"And Marí?"

"Sleeping," Lourdes said. "She's not in good shape."

Alberto took a deep breath. He leaned forward, off-balance. Lourdes helped him sit against the back of the chair. They made an interesting pair: *gusano y patriota,* the worm and the patriot.

He found enough energy to ask another question. "I still need to know what's next. Where do we go from here?"

They all looked at me.

# – Chapter 17 –
## ALL THIS DEATH

Meaningful sleep again eluded me. I nodded off for maybe an hour, woke up, tossed and turned for twenty minutes. Eventually I dozed off again for another hour. The bed was too soft, the blankets too bulky, the room too small. Tropical darkness closed in on me, my throat tightened, and I couldn't shake the sensation of suffocating.

Around four in the morning, I stood at the window. I wore only a T-shirt and boxer briefs, yet my skin was hot and sweaty. My three-day-old beard scratched my neck. The whiskers were hard as wire. Music continued to echo from the impromptu concert in the town center. A rooster crowed although the sun had not yet broken through the night.

A wild thought formed in my sleep-deprived brain. Which of my fellow travelers could I really trust? As if I expected the answer to be revealed, I pulled back the heavy drapes and stared at the courtyard through a thin sheer curtain. A light was on in Marita's room. I watched for five minutes. I thought she might also have trouble falling asleep. I imagined her crying over the murder of her husband. Maybe she prayed. Maybe she hoped to drink away the memory.

The door to her room opened. Alberto inched out of the doorway. He made sure no one else was in the courtyard, then he took Marita's hands in his own and rubbed them as though they were cold. They hugged, quickly, without emotion. He limped as quietly as he could, but I could hear him shuffling through the courtyard. He passed Lourdes' room, paused, raised his hand to the doorknob, changed his mind and finished walking to his own room. A light turned on, then out seconds later. The light in Marita's room faded about a minute later.

I slipped on my pants. Sleep was impossible. I walked outside with the hope that the night air would jumpstart my Circadian rhythms. I lit the cigar Margarita had given me. The smoke was sweet. I looked up at the stars and the cloud-shrouded moon. I imagined where I stood on the Cuban map, but wasn't sure.

"Can't sleep?" Marita's voice surprised me. I hadn't seen her standing in a corner of the courtyard. "Nor can I," she added.

The moonlight washed out her tired face. In the glow of the night she'd regained a hint of the beauty I'd seen at El Supremo. She left her corner and swayed to me. She stopped when she bumped into my shoulder.

"You've been drinking," I said.

"I am always drinking. I never stop. You want a drink? In my room."

"No, thanks. You should go to sleep. It's very late."

"Come with me, Gus. I need company."

She brought her mouth to my lips and kissed me. The tip of her tongue rubbed against my teeth, then my own tongue. I wanted to stay with the kiss, but I pulled away.

"You don't need me. You need sleep."

She grabbed the cuff of my shirt. I pulled away again. I tossed the cigar.

"Go to your room, Marita."

She bent over, groaned, then straightened her body. The look she gave me was a menagerie of lust, regret, anger.

I walked back to my room. From my window I looked over the courtyard. I saw no one.

꙳ ꙳ ꙳

Margarita's cook, Josefa, served us a breakfast of coffee, scrambled eggs and sliced mangoes. The short, black woman said that Margarita usually came down from her room around ten in the morning, so we were on our own for two hours, at least.

The mother, Constancia, sat in the courtyard reading a book. She ignored us and Josefa, who badgered the old woman to come in to eat.

We didn't do much talking. Virgilio had joined Juanito during the night, but I expected him at any time to continue his bodyguard responsibilities.

Lourdes still had her arm wrapped, Alberto continued to drag his injured leg, and Marita sat glumly in her chair, subdued and alone. She ignored me.

"I thought about our situation," I said when the coffee hit my brain.

I tried to sound professional, as though my words came from thoughtful planning and not the fevered dreams of an anxious and isolated Northside Denver *cholo*.

"It's a mistake for us to just sit here, waiting, not doing anything. Someone's trying to kill us because of the money. If we get the money back to the States, out of Cuba at least, that should end this. I don't know who is after the money, not sure it really matters. But staying here, as still targets, doesn't feel good. We have to do something. We can't let the killers control what we do."

"You may be right," Lourdes said. "I haven't had time to think this through. Everything's happened too fast since Hoochie was shot. But Detective Solís wants us here. He doesn't want us exposing ourselves."

Alberto grunted. "I could care less what the so-called policeman wants," he said. "I'm ready to go home. I need to leave before this country kills me. Let's get the money and take it to your friends, Lourdes, so that they can return it, the same way they brought it into Cuba. It can be waiting for me when I finally get back to Denver."

She set down her cup and glared at her brother. "Why would the money be waiting for you?" Lourdes asked. Her face flushed with anger. "You know it's Joaquín's money. It's always Joaquín's money that saves you, rescues you from your latest mistake, your latest crisis."

Alberto shook his head.

"Don't deny it," Lourdes said. "There are too many examples. How much did he give you for the pregnant intern? Or the accident in the mountains when you were drunk? How much has he paid over the years for your *bobadas*, your mistakes? And now these gambling debts—to Almeida of all people!"

Alberto continued to shake his head.

"You have no shame, Alberto, no shame."

He tried to laugh off his sister's words, but the sound he made was a pathetic squeak. Marita frowned at him, Lourdes stared through him.

"The money will go back to Joaquín," Lourdes finally said. "Where it came from."

Alberto managed to speak. "No need to talk about my business, Lourdes. You not only don't understand my business, you don't understand my arrangement with Kino. I'm his partner, I can . . . "

"Partner!" Lourdes shouted. "You're his obligation, his charity case. You're nothing but a glorified servant, and that's only because he takes pity on you, keeps you around so you don't starve. And you pay him back by causing all this . . . " she choked on her words. "All this death. *Toda esta muerte.* Carlito. Esteban. Even Hoochie."

"Those are not on me," Alberto said, his voice rising in volume with each word. "How could you think that? I was in the van when it was ambushed, remember? Look at me! I'm practically a cripple. You're talking crazy."

"It's the truth. You know it, Joaquín knows it, I know it."

"You don't know a damn thing! *No sabes nada.* Kino needs me. He relies on me, he . . . "

"Face the truth! Be a man for once in your life. Accept your responsibility."

Alberto stood up from his untouched coffee. He looked at me, then at Marita. He shook his head and again tried to laugh off Lourdes' condemnations. And again, it did not happen. Still shaking his head, he bolted from the table. He almost ran to his room.

The two women kept their eyes on their food. Perhaps they were embarrassed for Alberto, perhaps for themselves. I tried to drink the coffee, but the sweet, thick liquid sat at the back of my throat.

"We'll give Federico another day or two," Lourdes finally said. "If we don't hear from him, we'll return to La Habana. Then you should leave, Gus. Take Alberto back to your country. I'll have the money returned to Joaquín. You're right, the threat will be over when the money is gone."

"I'll stay as long as you need me," I said.

"You can't stay in Cuba forever. You've done more than you signed up for. No, you should leave. Take my brother back to his country, as he says. Take him back where he belongs. He's not a Cuban any longer. Take him home."

"If that's what you want."

She nodded, then gathered the cups and remaining spoons and forks still on the table. She carried the utensils to the over-sized metal sink. She wobbled with uncertainty, then leaned against the counter.

Marita hardly moved. Her eyes looked down at the floor, and I couldn't be certain that she was still conscious.

The silence of both women filled the space entirely. I left them to it and walked through the courtyard to Alberto's room. He let me in and I sat on the only chair. He perched on the edge of his bed.

"I apologize for that scene with my sister," he said not looking at me.

I shook my head to mean he didn't owe me an apology, but he didn't see it.

"She's been like that since we were children. Maybe it started when Hoochie's brother was killed. She was closer to that family than Kino or I were." He stretched his neck. "She doesn't understand me, or the relationship I have with Kino. She's always on me about that, but Kino needs me. You realize that, don't you?"

"He said something like that when he hired me," I said. "He wanted me to get rid of the threat not only to him, but to you and Lourdes. He was very concerned about the both of you."

I didn't answer his question, but he didn't seem to notice.

"He's the ultimate big brother. He's never failed to look out for Lourdes and me."

"The money is his?" I said it casually, as though I knew the answer and it was of only minor importance.

"It can be seen that way. We are business partners, and I am entitled to certain profits and returns on my investments. But the actual cash that we were going to turn over to Almeida? That came from Kino—which the Commissioner's Office can never know. Of course, I have to pay him back out of my share of the partnership." He caught himself. "Well, I guess I don't now since it'll be returned soon."

"Lourdes wants us to stay here for two more days. Then we leave, Solís' blessing or no. You and I will fly to Denver. That's the end of this."

He rubbed his hands together. "Yes, at last. The end of this . . . what would you call it? An adventure? Your Cuban adventure? I can't wait to leave."

He looked more like the man I'd met in the Los Angeles airport.

"At least," I said, "I hope it's the end."

"What do you mean? Why wouldn't it be?"

His regained self-assurance slipped away in the brisk morning air. He returned to the deflated, tired man who'd come to Trinidad from a Havana hospital.

I considered a dozen different answers to his questions. "Sorry. That's just me. Sometimes I see only the negative. My sister says I'm too cynical."

"Yes," he said. "I know what you mean. It might be the Hispanic in us. We can be extremely cynical."

Yeah, that might've been it.

꒰꒰꒰ ꒰꒰꒰ ꒰꒰꒰

My stomach started to feel queasy the third day in Trinidad. I blamed Josefa and her scrambled eggs. Or maybe it was the occasional glass of tap water I sipped when no bottled water was handy. Lourdes gave me a half-filled tin of red pills to thwart oncoming diarrhea, and whatever they were, they plugged me up good. The nausea remained, though, and I knew I had a fever. But I convinced everyone that I could travel, that I wouldn't be an obstacle to a quick return trip.

We set out for the city at night. Juanito's van was packed with Lourdes, Marita, Alberto, Virgilio and me. Occasionally, Juanito would point out something on the landscape or comment on the rough road. The passengers were silent, caught up in their own drama of grief, pain or whatever it was that somehow culminated in that van ride back to Havana.

Most of the time I slept on the last seat. The journey turned into agony for me. I suffered cramps and hot flashes. I sweated, soaked my shirt and I couldn't eat anything—not that I even wanted to.

I'd occasionally raise my head and look out through the van windows. No street or highway lights. Darkness always surrounded us. Then we'd round a random curve and our headlights would confront a group of people standing on the edge of the road, waiting for something. A bus most likely. The van's headlights would shine on the group and Juanito would speed by, only inches away from exhausted-looking women and children clinging to the legs of their parents. It happened several times.

Or, out of nowhere, a jogger in running shorts and a T-shirt would appear in the headlights. He'd look back over his shoulder at us, but he wouldn't move over.

Juanito expertly maneuvered around joggers, bicyclists, hitch-hikers and walkers trying to make it home from work. The darkness of the countryside was extreme. The van's headlights were not enough to light up the road completely, or to warn others that we were coming through, but Juanito's driving skills made up for the bad headlamps.

We stopped at the beach where I'd met the young fans of rock 'n roll on our way to Trinidad. Everyone else climbed out to stretch their legs. Officially, the beach was closed, but Juanito ignored the signs, doused his lights and parked close enough to the shore that

I heard the waves breaking against the rough and rocky ledges. I hadn't planned to leave my perch in the back, but I changed my mind with the hope that the salty air might make me feel better.

I stumbled along a path that wound through palm trees and knee-high grass. Off to my left I heard Lourdes and Alberto arguing. Their rapid conversation continued the fight they'd started back in Trinidad. I veered to my right and found myself on a flat outcrop of sea-battered rock that hung over the swirling water. Sea water sprayed me. I breathed deeply, waiting for something, anything to cure me.

The black ocean contrasted sharply with the star-filled sky and the almost full moon. I stood on the rock and sucked in the smell and taste of salt water and verdant jungle. The angry voices of Lourdes and Alberto bounced up at me from the water's edge.

I heard someone tripping on the rocks nearby. It was a woman, and she mumbled unintelligible words. I squinted to bring the figure into focus.

Marita made her way slowly along the shore. She continued to mumble with the rhythm of a prayer. She stood in water that rolled around her ankles. Behind her, the beach glistened with yellow brilliance. She looked up at the sky, and I thought I heard her moan, as though the silver moon had blinded her, as though the stars had stabbed her heart.

I thought of the golden nights I'd experienced in Cuba. I tried to recall their beauty and promise. I couldn't find the gold anymore, only fake gold leaf.

I watched the tormented Marita walk into the water. She almost lost her step when a wave slapped against her thighs. She kept walking into the sea.

I didn't yell at her, didn't call for help. I didn't move, didn't try to stop her. She advanced, and the water whirled around her chest.

"Marita!" Virgilio hollered from the shore.

She jerked her head, tried to turn around and then she disappeared into the wet darkness.

Virgilio ran into the sea. He kept shouting her name.

Lourdes and Alberto hollered back.

"*¿Qué es? ¿Qué pasa?*"

I ran to the path, turned to where I'd seen Virgilio and stopped at the shoreline. I couldn't see anything in the blackness.

Lourdes and Alberto ran up behind me.

"What happened?" Lourdes asked.

"Marita," I said. "She went under. Virgilio's out there, somewhere."

"What? We have to help him," Alberto shouted.

"Neither of you are in any shape for that," I said.

I stepped toward the sea. The cold water shocked me, and again I felt queasy. I stopped.

Virgilio's head bobbed on the water. He held Marita by one arm.

# Part Three

# - Chapter 18 -
## NEAT AND SWEET

"Aw shit, Sherlock. You would've let her drown?"

Jerome's anger was never below the surface. He preferred it out in the open so the target of his ill-will would be clear about where he stood. It was my turn to wear the bullseye.

"I wish you'd quit calling me that."

"Homie don't play that, eh?"

"It's not funny."

"Beside the point. I repeat, you would've let her drown?"

"I didn't say that. I said I hesitated."

"You had to think over whether you should save a suicidal *cubana* from drowning in the Bay of Pigs?" He kept shaking his head.

"When you put it like that, it sounds bad."

"How else would you put it?"

He wasn't going to let it go. I'd been in Denver for a week, had convinced myself that I was back to my old self. Of course, I never figured out what my new self was supposed to be. I hoped I had left him in Cuba. I thought I should talk with Jerome about what happened in Havana and Trinidad. It didn't take long for me to regret my invitation.

"There's no good way to put it," I conceded. "You're right. At the time, I was suspicious of everyone. I was exhausted, sick, maybe delirious. Dehydrated and on some kind of communist medication. I think those red pills were designed to poison Americans. I'd been shot at and tortured, I . . . "

"You making excuses?" he interrupted.

"I'll stop if you stop asking me about it. It happened, I'm not denying it. You will think what you want. Can't help that."

"Okay, Sherlock. No more about your less than shining hour. Go on with your story."

Jerome had come at me hard about my lack of intervention when Marita tried to drown her grief and pain. I expected no less from him, but I wanted Jerome to react to what happened in Cuba. I needed his knowledge, his awareness. He had to put it in perspective for me. Jerome was good at that, so, the hassle was worth it.

His left arm still trembled, his fingers shook and his gait had become stiffer. He walked with a forced lunge, almost like Frankenstein's Monster. But his attitude was a hundred percent improved. He'd settled into a routine that included a healthier diet and several exercise classes each week, as well as a yoga session that he said he attended because of the young and flexible black woman who taught the class. Of course, he had to say that to save face. Not too many old-timer Northsiders were into yoga. Whatever the reason, he was in a better place, mentally. He said he was "just living life, like always."

"The exercise classes must be helping," I said.

"Yes, they seem to be. The only thing is . . . "

"What? There a problem?"

"It's just, I'm always the only Chicano. There must be hundreds of Latinos, men *and* women, with Parkinson's in Denver. But I never see them. Not in class or support group or at my doctor's office. I don't know why that is. These classes are cheap, some are free or take donations. Why don't the *raza* take care of themselves? I honestly believe these exercises do more for me than most of the meds they use on this disease."

"You don't like the people you train with?"

"Nah, that ain't it. Those people are good, great even. We're all in the same boat. There's lawyers, judges, teachers, dentists, museum volunteers . . . people, man. All kinds. They treat me decent, welcomed me to the PD world. I'd just like to see more *gente* participate. That's all I'm saying."

"Yeah, that's a mystery. Maybe they don't get the word, the info. And some of the elders aren't used to group exercise. It takes a lot to get an old Mexican into a gym."

"The senior centers I've looked at are busy with old people . . . Latino, white, you name it. So, I don't think that's it. They're not necessarily exercising, but they're involved, know what I mean? What you said about not knowing about the classes, that might be something. My doctor didn't say nothing about the Parkinson's Association and its classes when he gave me the diagnosis. Or he might have said something, but I was still too shocked, or in denial, to hear him. I kind of blanked out after he said 'Parkinson's.' Anyhow, I had to dig into the Internet to make that connection. But once I did, it was all there. Class schedules, fees. *Todo.* Everything I needed to know."

"Maybe you should spread the word."

"Maybe. I'll think about that."

I knew he would, and if he came up with a plan, I'd help however I could.

"Enough of that. More on your tropical nightmare."

He already knew the broad outline of my time on the island. I'd given that to him on the phone when I called with my new cell. I never found the phone I carried to Cuba. Our face-to-face was meant to fill in the details so he could tell me what he thought about the drama.

"Kino called earlier from Phoenix, said that the police, meaning Detective Solís, put the blame for everything on the two lowlifes who tried to convince me that they were with the U.S. Embassy. Apparently, they escaped from the Havana jail, where they'd been on ice."

"They were in jail?"

"Yeah. Since the night I took them on a wild goose chase to where I ran into that damn ox and Lourdes' men surprised us."

Jerome laughed.

"But then they escaped? From a Cuban jail?"

"That's the story. Funny how that worked out."

We both shook our heads.

"It is what it is. Lourdes passed the news on to Kino, then he called me. Solís trapped the pair two nights ago in a warehouse by the docks. In the shoot-out—surprise—Eddie and her partner,

Mario Faustino, ended up dead. I don't feel too bad about that outcome. That woman wanted to hurt me."

"So, that's it?" Jerome asked. "Everything tied up neat and sweet, with two fall guys ready-made?" He grinned like one of Corrine's Day of the Dead sugar skulls.

"What can I say? Justice was served, apparently. Solís' theory . . . the one he laid out for Lourdes . . . is that the two knuckleheads heard about this big chunk of change coming from the States. Maybe not much by U.S. criminal standards, but a pretty big deal in Cuba. Eddie and Faustino worked for Hoochie in the past, and Solís thinks someone from Hoochie's crew tipped them off, probably the guy who shot Hoochie and then was shot himself."

"Could be. Nothing like half-a-mil to test one's loyalty."

"There's more. The genius who called herself Eddie decided she wanted a piece of the money when she learned it was coming. No, that's not right. She wanted it all. She and Faustino set up the ambush, my kidnapping, the hit on Hoochie, even the torching of Lourdes' house."

"Busy little lowlifes."

"For sure. Like they say in Cuba: 'It's complicated'. If Eddie and Faustino put it together, they lost control quickly. Nothing worked. The ambush killed our driver and wounded Lourdes and Alberto, but the thieves didn't touch the money. They grabbed me and did their silly performance, but . . . "

"No money."

"*Correcto*. Their last gasps were the attacks on Hoochie and Lourdes' house."

"That part I don't get," Jerome said. "Why go after Lourdes' house? She wasn't there, and the money was being delivered to Hoochie. They had a hitman in place. What's the point?"

"With Eddie and Faustino, no telling, but my guess is they were being extra careful. What if Lourdes didn't have the money when we met up with Hoochie? Maybe she had to feel him out first. Make sure she could trust him."

"Your friends, Eddie and Mario, target her place too, in case she left the money in her house when she was supposed to be paying off Hoochie? Nothing like overkill."

"I tell you, they were idiots. But that overkill resulted in Lourdes losing a good man that night. Sánchez was more than just her house guard. She took it hard."

"And still no money for the bad guys."

His left foot rhythmically tapped the floor. It didn't look like he was aware of the movement.

"It's back in Kino's bank account?" he asked.

"He didn't tell me, except to say that it had been returned. He thanked me for my services and had his agent deliver my paycheck. That's sitting in *my* checking account as we speak."

"He paid you for this?"

I assumed he was joking. "You're still not funny."

"Whatever. How's the ballplayer doing? He still uptight about his brother's fuck-ups?"

"Hard to say. He sounded okay, almost. Talked like it was just another *telenovela*."

"He has to be pleased with the way it came down. The bad guy is gone, forever, and the money is back in the States. The heat's off him, his brother and his sister. All it cost was what he paid you, peanuts in the big picture, considering what was at stake."

"People were killed, Jerome."

"You think he's affected by that? I'd bet your paycheck that Kino Machaco didn't know any of the folks who bought it while you were in Cuba. Collateral damage. I'm not criticizing him, just saying that's the way it is."

"Could be. But he's having a terrible spring training. Guess there's speculation that he's injured somehow, so probably no connection to Cuba. Guy's not hitting anything."

"But he still gets paid. Right?"

"You know how it works."

"Like everything else. People with money make money. People without end up paying."

He'd said that before, so I didn't respond.

"Tell the truth," he said, "I'm more concerned about you. You saw a lot of action in Cuba: you were sick, people dying, bloody shootings, your fun time with Eddie and Faustino. You sure *you're* okay?"

"Yeah, why wouldn't I be? You and I have been through worse."

"Maybe. It can add up, though, then hit all at once. You ought to take a vacation, get some down time."

"As if. Nah, bro, I'm good."

"If you say so."

"Right. No worries."

He adjusted his posture by straightening his back.

"Seriously," I asked, "what do you think of all this?"

He grabbed his left thigh with both of his hands and the tapping foot stopped.

"It kind of makes sense, the way the detective is thinking. Eddie and Mario might not have been Bonnie and Clyde, but then, even Bonnie and Clyde ended up in the same place as your friends. Dead from cop bullets. I'm saying it could've gone down that way."

"But?"

"But I doubt it. That's too much drama, too many details to sweat, just for a big payday. Your friends might have been attracted to the bag of money, and they might have seriously thought about jumping in after it. But when they realized they had to actually plan something, and they had to take on this Hoochie guy and his organization, well, I get the impression they most likely weren't up to it."

"I know what you mean."

Years before, when Jerome and I were different people, we talked a few times about a "big job," a heist that would set us up for life. I saw then that he was meticulous, smart, and that if anyone could pull off a so-called big job, it was Jerome. He was the type of man who could've taken the money from Lourdes, Hoochie or me, and there wouldn't have been any dead drivers or house guards, and no shoot-out with cops in a dark and isolated warehouse. Eddie and Faustino were not Jerome.

He continued. "The police were pressured by the government. They needed to clean up the mess quickly, especially with the looser restrictions on travel to Cuba. Too many tourist dollars and euros that might vanish if Cuba's seen as a violent, crime-ridden island."

"They used what they had on hand: Eddie and Faustino."

"Yup. They got you and Lourdes out of the way, to avoid embarrassing questions or, worse, a dead American or dead pillar of the community. And you know there was more going on than you could see. It's almost too personal."

"Yeah, I got that, too. It wasn't only about the money. These people had a long history of bumping into each other's lives since they were kids. Up close and intimate. I think personal had to be a big part of it, whatever it was."

"Well, there you go," he said.

"There I go where?"

Jerome stood up and slipped into his red nylon jacket that made him look like Sal Mineo from a 1950s delinquent movie. A grandfatherly Mineo. He did it awkwardly, with some real difficulty. He had to tug on the jacket to straighten it over his torso. But I knew I shouldn't offer to help.

"There's two base reasons for the shit that happens between people, Gus. Well, three, really. I always overlook the addiction to power, mainly because that's something I've never been interested in, at least interested enough to risk another prison stretch."

He raised the collar of his jacket to complete the effect.

"You know this how?"

"Hard experience. I'm like the insurance guy on TV. I know a thing or two because I've seen a thing or two."

That made me smile. "And the other two reasons?" I asked, although I thought I knew what he was going to say.

"First. Follow the money. Who wanted it more than anything?"

"And?"

"Love's a bitch."

# - Chapter 19 -
## SCORPION WINGS

That evening, I made my way to Corrine's house. It was a trip I wasn't all that eager to take. She'd invited me for dinner and to "talk about something you started." She didn't explain, but I accepted the invite. I had to. She was my older sister, the head of the family, my savior—more than once. She had a right to know what her way-cray bro was up to, and to chew my ass out, if that was necessary. I had to believe it was for my own good.

Besides, she was bigger than me.

I lived in a stucco house in Wheat Ridge, on the western edge of Denver. It was about twenty minutes from Corrine's when traffic was decent. Denver proper had gentrified itself out of my price range, and I figured that was Denver's loss. At my first opportunity I moved to the rather static municipality that mixed with ever-growing Denver like balsamic vinegar on olive oil. The house was small, drafty and creaky. The front yard was about three feet wide, and the backyard didn't exist because the landlord, Rudy Padilla, affectionately known as "Rude the Crude" to his many tenants, kept a locked storage unit at the rear of the house that extended from the kitchen window to the alley fence. When I moved in six months before, Rudy told me to never mess with his shed. I didn't intend to, and I let him know, but he growled like he didn't believe me.

The house wasn't much, but it was a giant step for me. I'd been crashing on a cot in Corrine's cluttered basement since I'd been released from prison. Thankfully, that part of my life was over. My detective business had taken hold and business improved each month. As I said before, most of my work was grunt level, certainly nothing glamorous. It was all good, though. I paid my rent when it was due, I drove a used Ford pickup, a

120

dozen years old but in good shape, and I no longer had to worry about making life less than pleasant for Corrine, who perched upstairs like a wary momma cat guarding her babies. I was on my own.

Corrine and I talked briefly on the phone when I'd returned from Cuba, and she knew a sanitized version of my adventure, but I guessed that she wanted to get the full story and then rip into me with "told-you-so" and "you-never-learn."

I pushed her doorbell button right at six-thirty. She let me in and I smelled roast chicken, fresh *frijoles* and garlic. She gave me a nod of the head as a greeting and I followed her to the living room, where I encountered the first surprise of the night.

Sofía Santisteven, otherwise known as Soapy, rested on Corrine's couch. She held a glass of wine and looked very comfortable. A plastic red portfolio covered with skateboarding stickers rested against the side of her leg.

Soapy must have been all of twenty-three years old. I'd met her when I sat in on a computer course at the Community College of Denver, shortly after I walked out of the pen. She taught the class even though she was younger than most of her students. It was basic techie stuff, but it was apparent that she and computers had a special relationship. And besides, I needed the basic stuff.

In class, she was funny and patient. She explained the course content in ways that even I could understand, the guy who had trouble with pocket calculators in my North High algebra class. Like the ancient song says: "Don't know what a slide rule is for."

She laughed in my face when I asked her out. "I don't date my students," she said. She turned her back and packed her laptop. "Or ex-cons," she added.

Despite her harsh put-down, we gradually became friends when she saw that I was serious about learning what she taught.

Since then, I'd hired her a few times when my clients required her type of help. She worked with me on cases involving identity theft, computer scams and missing persons. I hadn't asked her out again.

"Hey, Soapy," I said. "Never would've guessed that you'd be here. In fact, I'm surprised you even know my sister."

"Small world, eh?"

She moved over on the couch to make room for me.

"We met a while back, right when you left the country," Corrine said. "All because of you, Gus."

I sat down on the end of the couch and waited for an explanation.

"Sofía called me," Corrine said. "She said she was working for you, something you left with her before your trip. A client you didn't have time for, and you thought she had the skills to help the guy."

"Leo Hudgens," Sofía said. "You remember him?"

I nodded. I'd put the man behind the name out of my thinking while I was busy in Cuba, but as soon as Sofía mentioned him, his ugly story flooded back with more details than I needed or wanted.

"The homeless ex-cop," I said. "He wanted to clear his conscience about the death of a kid that he and his ex-partner were involved in, years ago. He asked me to track down the partner, and . . . bring him in, I guess. Yes, I remember. But what's that got to do with you, Corrine?"

Corrine got a worried look on her face. "Just a sec," she said. She rushed into the kitchen.

"I checked out Hudgens before I talked with him," Sofía said. "He had a good record as a cop before he teamed up with Alito, before the death of Leon Parker. He was heavily involved in community affairs."

She opened the plastic envelope and pulled out a file folder. She scanned it, then handed it to me.

"He volunteered for programs with teens, gang members, old folks, schools. He was into a lot of stuff. Good stuff. I felt sorry for the guy when I saw how it turned for him, how he wasted his life."

The file folder held several loose pages of notes, copies of documents and email messages. Everything was dated, and most was in chronological order. Soapy's handwritten entries were neat and precise.

Corrine reappeared. She dried her hands with a kitchen towel. My sister gave me the second surprise of the night.

"I've known Leo for years," Corrine said. "He and I worked together on an after-school basketball project for middle-schoolers from Globeville, Swansea and Elyria. He was a good man: honest, devoted to the kids, hard-working. We did some good things together. So much so that I forgot he was a cop. It was irrelevant."

That statement threw me. Corrine and police officers did not get along. That was a certainty. And here she was, practically calling him a friend.

"But he dropped out of everything after the incident with Parker and Delly Thomas. I hadn't seen him since then. Not until Soapy got us together."

"You talked with Hudgens?" I asked.

"Several times," Corrine answered. "We've been working hard on finding his old partner, Alito. A lot of hours, Gus."

"Where are you doing all this work?"

"I have a key to your office, remember? And sometimes we get together here, in my house."

"Really?"

"Yes. You might want to know that he spent a night or two here, sleeping in your old bed in the basement."

"Damn."

"Like I said. We have a lot of hours on this. You owe me."

"Take that to your old pal, Hudgens. Far as I know, working for him is pro bono. Free."

"He's got money,"

"I forgot. His stash in the plastic bag. He hasn't shot it all into his arm?"

"He's trying to maintain," Soapy said. "Corrine's helping him clean up, in all ways that clean can mean."

"Forgive me if I'm not impressed. The guy killed a kid and then covered it up. He might have been a good policeman once, but he ended up being a dirty cop. You realize that if we really help him and he comes clean, as you say, he's going to prison. Your helping him means his days outside are numbered. And then he'll be an ex-cop in prison. You know what *that* means. Does he understand that?"

"We talked about the consequences," Corrine said. "He's reconciled to his fate. He needs this, Gus. The accident ruined his life. I'm going to help him."

"Accident? Is that what he calls it?"

"That's what *I* call the death of Leon Parker," Corrine said.

That's when the third surprise hit me, and I grasped what had happened. My world had changed, and I almost missed my cue. Instead of Corrine rapping my knuckles because of my misadventure in Cuba, I was the one who could lay out the negatives of her planned actions. I could warn her, play the role of younger but wiser brother. I almost felt warm and cuddly. I would be the one down the road who would be entitled to say, "I told you so."

"You want to help," I said. "I get it. You'll do what you can. I turned him over to Soapy, so I must be willing to do something for him. But he's not sleeping at my place, and he's paying our expenses, at least. If he doesn't turn himself in, whether we find Alito or not, I will. He's going to face up to what he did, one way or the other."

"That's all he wants," Soapy said.

I didn't blame her for siding with Corrine. Soapy was young, idealistic and eager to save the world. Corrine knew better.

The universe had turned upside down and was threatening to twist inside out. My sister, the activist, the community leader, a person who helped organize fundraisers for Black Lives Matter, now took up the cause of a policeman who admitted to killing a black youth. I worried that she would tarnish her hard-won reputation among the progressives and militants who sometimes gathered at her house. They could be a merciless, unforgiving crowd. I worried, but Corrine didn't bother about such things, she simply did what she thought was right. This time, she would do what she could to help the homeless haunted white man gain a bit of peace, bring him closure, which really meant finding a way to pay for his crimes. I couldn't argue with that conclusion, but her friends might not see it in the same way.

"Guess we'll find out," I said. "But when this goes haywire, when Hudgens is off the tracks, when he's screwed up everything you tried to do for him, remember what I said tonight."

I couldn't help myself. I enjoyed the role. I smiled, inside, and Corrine grimaced like a bug had flown in her mouth.

"I get it," Corrine said. "You don't trust the man."

"No, that's not it. I trust him. I trust him to let you both down and to betray himself. He's weak. That much I know already. When he lined up with Alito, he revealed the true Leo Hudgens. He may not have liked what he saw, but he rolled with it. That's who this guy is."

"You're wrong, Gus," Corrine said. "All we can do is wait and see."

"As always," I said.

In prison, I read hundreds of books. I forgot many of them, remembered only bits and pieces of others. But some stayed with me, as if carved in my hard head by a laser. One of those was a slim volume of old Mexican *dichos*, folk sayings. Each page had a saying, in English and Spanish, and a black-and-white drawing representing the lesson of the particular *dicho*. The book was put together by a professor of Chicano/a Studies from the University of Texas at El Paso, and his wife—a graphic artist. I forgot their names, but I memorized all one hundred and thirteen *dichos*, in English *and* Spanish.

When Corrine said, "You're wrong, Gus," I thought of one of my favorite *dichos: "Dios no les dio alas a los alacranes.* God did not give wings to scorpions."

"Let's eat." Soapy said.

# – Chapter 20 –
## CAD

The next day I waited in my office for Soapy, Corrine and Hudgens. When Soapy called to let me know they were coming in, she promised to have good news.

Unfortunately, that morning's *Denver Post* didn't have the same beat.

Major League Baseball was gearing up for a new season in a few weeks, but the Rockies were not favored to repeat as National League Western Division champs. Key players were injured, the pitching was weak and the owners were at odds with the manager. Most important, the team's superstar, Joaquín Machaco, was mired in the worst slump of his career. On the other hand, these were only Cactus League games, so no one panicked. Yet. "After all," the reporter wrote, maybe with more optimism than was defensible, "Kino always starts slow."

Kino was the new face of the Rockies. In the past few years, as he began to make his mark on the record books, Denver grew up in terms of baseball. It wasn't enough for the team owners to offer a beautiful summer day, a great view from the stadium seats, over-priced beer, Rocky Mountain Oysters and a mediocre team. Fans had become accustomed to winning, and now nothing less would satisfy.

Kino was a winner—at least, he had been. His wide smile and gleaming bald head were plastered all over Denver: sides of buses, banners along the streets to the stadium, Coors beer posters. He regularly visited schools, children's hospitals and senior centers. Everyone loved him.

No matter. The consensus, outside of Denver, was that the Cuban star had lost a step, and he didn't have enough left in his tank to again take the Rockies over the hump. *Wait and see,* like Corrine said.

In other news, the racist President of the good ol' U.S.A. appeared to have lost his final grip on sanity. Again. The man was an international joke, and I couldn't stomach any more stories about his outrageous charade. He was, after all, only pretending to be the leader of the free world. It was obvious everything he did was about protecting his own bottom line. That was the American Way, wasn't it? I didn't need to read more of his ridiculous tweets or see more videos that documented his unfitness for the office he held.

The final story I read before I turned to the crossword was about the I-25 shooter. He'd struck again. A motorcyclist had been shot up north near the Wyoming state line, when traffic was light. He'd crashed his bike into a gulley where he bled to death. His body was found hours later by a rancher checking his fence line.

That was enough news for me.

I stared at the crossword for what seemed like hours. It was from the previous Sunday. I'd started it but hadn't finished. From Sunday's paper I worked the *L.A. Times* puzzle, and that morning not even the hints made sense. Forget about any answers.

My mind wouldn't focus. I wandered back to Cuba and memories of the people I'd met: Lourdes and her inherent strength; Marita, beautiful and in pain; insensitive Alberto. Then I thought about Hudgens and what I might say when I saw him. I watched Marita walk into the ocean again. I heard Lourdes scream when the fake police shot our driver, Carlito. I listened to Alberto's phony bravado in the face of Lourdes' condemnation. I thought of these things and others, and so I didn't find the calm the puzzle usually created. Sweat collected in my underarms and, for a second, I couldn't catch my breath as bloody images from Cuba paraded through my head. I became irritated with the news, the puzzle and the meeting. The last thing I read before I threw the paper in the trash can was question ten—down of the crossword, four letters: *Cad.* I tried to not take it personally.

Hudgens walked into my office about fifteen minutes later. Corrine and Soapy were with him. He'd been shaved and showered and given a good haircut and clean clothes. He mumbled hello when he saw me, but his eyes would not connect with mine.

"Your office needs help," Corrine said. "A little bit of color would go a long way. Get rid of that beat-up cooler. Hang a picture or two."

"I haven't been thinking about interior decoration," I said. "I'm more about spending my time trying to make a buck or two, enough to pay the rent. That and attracting a better breed of clientele. But I'll mention your ideas to Goldstein. I'm sure, he'll agree." Sam Goldstein, retired accountant, owned the building.

"Think long-term, Gus. A nice looking and comfortable office might attract customers. If I didn't know you, I might worry that this is just a front for a serial killer, or something worse. Needs a little joy, if you ask me."

She wanted to be funny, to soften the mood, but it didn't work.

"Not asking. The people who come to me aren't looking for joy. They want photos of their wife having sex with the plumber, or a subpoena served on the guy who knocked out my client's teeth with a tire iron, or proof that their thirteen-year-old daughter's online boyfriend is really three times her age. No joy in any of that."

"Yikes, Gus," Soapy said, "lighten up. Oh my god."

"It's okay, Sofía," Corrine said. "I'll come in here when he's not around . . . maybe in jail again . . . and I'll fix the place up. Then he'll thank me."

"Don't mess with my stuff," I said. They were futile words.

"You're in an ugly mood," Soapy said. "You not sleeping again?"

"I sleep fine," I lied. "If anything's bugging me, it's this guy." I pointed at Hudgens. "He's still walking around, free and upright, when he ought to be in prison."

"This is a mistake," Hudgens said.

He turned to the door. Corrine blocked his way.

"It will be okay," Corrine said. "Everyone sit down and let Sofía tell us what she's found. Relax, Gus. You started this when you asked Sofía to help. Now you have to finish it."

I didn't have enough chairs for the four of us. The building manager had a closet with a table and a half-dozen chairs in what he called the conference room. He'd given me a key, and I led the way down the dim hallway, past the deserted dentist office, the dark insurance company and the sullen and skittish collection agency receptionist who kept her door partially open.

Eventually, we sat at the conference table, one of us on each side. I felt uneasy, out of whack. Doubt about what I was doing ate at me like a parasitic worm sitting in my bowels.

"I just want to say that I appreciate all that you've done," Hudgens said. "You've done more than I expected or deserve. Thank you."

"Let's get on with this," I said.

Soapy arched her pierced eyebrows at Corrine.

"Well, it's good and bad," Soapy said. "The good is that Dominick Alito is still alive. He calls himself Don Allen these days, and for most of the past five, going on six years, he's lived in Long Beach, California, managing a restaurant for a cousin. Last year, that restaurant closed, and Don Allen dropped out of sight."

"But Soapy kept at it," Corrine said. "She's like a pitbull when she gets behind the computer."

"Good to know," I said. "He changed his name?"

"Yes, although I couldn't find a specific reason why he'd change his identity when he moved to California."

"Clean slate?" I asked, my eyes on Hudgens.

"Maybe," she said. "Whatever—I lost Alito's cyber trail, so I turned to the cousin who owned the restaurant, a guy named Tony DiNunzio, also known as Tony the Nun."

"You're joking," I said.

"Nope. That's his nickname, and not because he's a religious nut. Apparently, Mr. DiNunzio always dresses in black suits and white shirts. Gives him a Mother Superior kind of look. And it's not much of a stretch from DiNunzio to 'the nun.'"

"Not that I'd stereotype, but is this guy a mobster?" Corrine asked. "Organized crime?"

"I'd be willing to bet on it," Soapy answered. "He's never been convicted of anything more than a speeding ticket, but the FBI is very interested in him. I found lots of chatter and references about him from various law enforcement sources."

"I didn't know that Dominick was connected," Hudgens said. "Or about his cousin. We never talked about things like family."

"Both these guys vanished?" I asked.

"For a while. But I picked up the trail again when, just for grins, I ran a search of new incorporations in California, Nevada and Colorado after the closing of the Long Beach restaurant."

"Long-ass search," I said.

She nodded. "I didn't expect much, and it took a couple of hours, but I had to laugh when I saw the corporate filing for a place called 'The Sicilian Nun.'"

"That's funny, in a gangster way," Corrine said.

"The Sicilian Nun is a five-star restaurant, with a pricey menu and a reputation for authentic Sicilian and Mediterranean dishes. It's making plenty of money for the partners."

"The partners include DiNunzio and Alito, or Allen?" I asked.

"You better believe it," Soapy said. "Chairman of the Board of Directors is Anthony DiNunzio. Secretary and Treasurer of the Board is Mr. Donald Allen. There are others, but those two own the controlling share of the business."

"Alito must've invested money in the restaurant," Corrine said. "Where'd that come from?"

"That was harder to find out, but that's the thing about insurance companies. They don't like to pay claims, even those filed by their own customers. And if the customers fight back, and the company doesn't cave immediately, the fight over the claim creates several files and communication trails that eventually give up a truckload of information about the claim, the claimants and the resolution. It took several all-night trips through dozens of dull and arcane insurance files, but I learned that DiNunzio and Allen, or Alito, won their claim. They were paid a million bucks by the insurance company."

"Wow," I said. "There was more to the closing of the Long Beach restaurant?"

"It burned down." Soapy nodded enthusiastically as she spoke. She was in techie heaven, proud of what she could do with a computer and getting off on revealing her success to the rest of us.

"Gas leaks and hot grease don't mix. The cousins made a bundle."

"Good work, Soapy," Corrine said. "Where are these guys now? Where's this Sicilian Nun?"

"I'd say take a guess, but I can see that Gus is losing his patience, so I'll just say it. About sixty-five miles south of Denver, in the little burg of Old Colorado City, which is really the west side of Colorado Springs, between the Springs and Manitou. It's a small tourist collection of gift shops, art galleries and restaurants. A few blocks only. And the hottest place in Old Colorado City is a swanky, pricey joint called The Sicilian Nun. Only a little more than an hour away."

Hudgens finally stirred. "He's back in Colorado?" His pale skin lightened almost to transparency.

"He's obviously not worried about his past catching up to him," I said.

"What's the next step?" Corrine asked. "Don't tell me you're going to bring him in." She looked at me as she spoke.

Before I could respond, Hudgens said, "I'll get him."

Soapy, Corrine and I shook our heads in unison.

"No way," I said.

"Don't be a fool," Corrine said.

"We go to the police, like we planned," Soapy said. "Tell them your story. Let them deal with it."

Hudgens' head fell into his cupped hands. "That's not going to do anything. It's been years. Parker's death, that entire night, was investigated by the D.A. Nothing came of it then, nothing will now."

"You covered it up then," Corrine said. "You're making it right. The cops, D.A., somebody will believe you. You have no reason to lie. You're turning yourself in, for God's sake."

"I'll be confessing to a crime that officially doesn't exist. The Department and the District Attorney won't let me stir up trouble for something they locked away a long time ago. It's hopeless."

"You get cold feet?" I asked. "Now that we know where Alito is, you don't want to go through with it, is that it? You were a coward when you killed Leon Parker, and you're still one today."

He looked up at me. His eyes were raw, his lips thin and flat. "The police won't do anything to him." His weak voice barely carried across the table. "I'm too late. I'll tell what I know, but it won't make any difference. Guys like Alito never get what they deserve, only what they take."

"That may be," I said. "Except for you, Leo. I'm gonna make sure you get what's coming to you. You can count on that."

"Come on, Gus," Corrine said.

"Jesus," Soapy said.

I stood up. I couldn't take the enclosed room any more. My sister, Soapy and Hudgens pressed in on me. Again, I felt hot and disoriented.

"Where you going?" Corrine asked.

"I gotta get some air."

"We're not done, Gus," Corrine hollered at my back.

I stopped and turned around. "Figure it out. If this worthless piece of humanity is ready, I'll go with him to the police to tell his story. If he's not, I'll do it on my own."

I walked out of the room, caught the elevator and stumbled through the building's front door. I breathed as deeply as I could, leaning against a graffiti-covered wall. The trip to Cuba wasn't finished with me. Although I wanted to believe otherwise, I hadn't been the same since I'd returned. My hands shook, reminding me of Jerome, and I spiraled into gray nausea. My back slid down the wall until I sat on the sidewalk. Bloody and violent scenes from Cuba flooded around and through me. I couldn't move.

Corrine, Soapy and Hudgens found me about fifteen minutes later. Corrine pulled me from the sidewalk, then took me home.

# – Chapter 21 –
# THE RIGHT THING

After the meeting at my office, Corrine gave me something that knocked me out. I slept for seven hours.

I woke up groggy and hungry. I jogged a couple of miles around the neighborhood, made a big breakfast, ate half of it and then called Corrine. Figured I would try again to make sense out of what we were doing for Leo Hudgens. I went over everything I knew about the Hudgens job with her. She asked questions, made suggestions, told me what Hudgens wanted. In other words, everything that we should've talked about during our aborted meeting.

She let me know that Hudgens left some of his money in my office, "as a deposit for future services."

"He's going through with it after all?"

"Yes. Which means we have to be ready."

At the end of the call we had a plan.

"Where's Hudgens?" I asked. "Where will he be? I can pick him up."

"He can stay here," she said. "I'll keep an eye on him and make sure he's ready when you come for us. What do you think? About three, three-thirty?"

"Yeah, around three-thirty. Traffic is crazy that time of day. And if we want to be there with the dinner crowd, we should leave early."

"You're going on I-25?"

"If you're worried about the shooter, don't be. Thousands of people drive that highway every day without getting shot."

"And three people have died. Or is it four?"

"I can use highway eighty-three. Takes longer, though."

"We should consider it. We'll have Soapy and Hudgens in the car. We'll be responsible for them."

I agreed with my sister and said I'd see her the next afternoon.

Then I texted Jerome Rodríguez. I assumed he answered from his trendy coffee shop in the RiNo district of hipsterish Denver. We set a time to meet that evening.

I spent most of the day at my office. A few hours were rough. Anxiety built up in me again, and more than once I had to leave the building and walk a few blocks.

The Lewis Building, where I had my office, sat on a corner of South Broadway, several blocks from the Englewood city limit, further south, and Antique Row, to the north. A long way from Wheat Ridge. It wasn't convenient, but it was what I could afford. The building's history included a speakeasy in the basement during Prohibition and a high-tone bordello on the top floor in the fifties. The place had a checkered past, and that sealed the deal for me when I hunted for office space.

Englewood was another town like Wheat Ridge that had been swallowed by Denver without losing its formal status as a separate government. The area, nicknamed SoBo, was relatively untouched by the Denver construction spree and development mania. Old structures survived, such small businesses as car washes, dive bars and used car lots. When the detective racket slowed down, I sometimes spent too much time across busy Broadway in the Blind Bat, one of the joints that had been serving beer and live music since the turn of the century, a Denver rarity.

The day dragged on. When I could no longer take the gas fumes of Broadway traffic and I stopped walking in circles around SoBo, I busied myself with catching up on what I'd let pile up while I was in Cuba. I had bills to pay, invoices to mail and reports to write. Nothing I really wanted to do. More than once I nodded off at my desk. I didn't take that as a good sign. If I got serious about sleep and laid down on a bed, no doubt I'd toss and turn until I had to jump to my feet. I just couldn't win.

Around six-thirty, I hooked up with Jerome at his house.

The large Victorian looked almost the same as when I'd first stepped into the place years before. It sat on a hill near the Willis Case golf course. The yard was cluttered with various landscaping projects or repair jobs, all half-finished. Materials and tools were scattered everywhere. For a sec I flashed on the thought that Jerome would never finish the projects now that Parkinson's had become a part of his life.

The inside walls were covered with art, mostly Latino and Latina artists. Latinx artists, as Corrine would've said. At least one of the paintings was new to me. It was a colorful montage of superhero and cartoon characters, interspersed with iconic symbols of the Chicano Movement. Mickey Mouse pointed at César Chávez's silhouette; the *huelga* eagle tormented Batman; the brown power clenched fist gripped Bugs Bunny; and Quetzalcoatl, feathered serpent god of Mesoamerica, serenely looked over the mad scene. I knew without checking that the artist was Denver's Carlos Frésquez.

Jerome sat on his leather couch. A stack of books was perched on a small table next to the couch. His left foot tapped the carpet.

"There's beer in the fridge," he said.

I helped myself to a Bohemia, then sat on his recliner.

The place carried a bachelor vibe: dark colors, minimal knick-knacks, dusty shelves. It'd taken years for Jerome to finally own a home. He was entitled to keep it any way he wanted.

"You should've listened to me," Jerome said. "You need a vacation, a break. You're falling apart. I see it in your face."

"I don't get it," I said. "I was okay when I returned to Denver. Just tired."

"Shit builds up, then something triggers the anxiety and it lays you out."

"Must've been the meeting with Hudgens. That guy bugs the hell out of me."

"He's not my favorite either, but it sounds like he's trying to do the right thing. You gotta give him that."

Jerome and Corrine had talked earlier, so he knew the general outline of what we were up to and who the players were.

"Maybe. I find out for sure tomorrow. We're supposed to drive down to Springs, confront this Alito guy, then meet back up here with Denver cops."

"You want me to go with you?"

"Thanks, but Corrine and Soapy are tagging along. I don't think they trust me to be alone with Hudgens."

"Corrine is the smart one of your parents' kids."

"Screw you. Anyway, it's mostly her plan. If it goes like we think, Hudgens gets arrested, and the police go after Alito for assorted crimes."

"This Alito could be dangerous, or his cousin, or the guys who work for them. You sure I shouldn't come along? And why meet with Alito anyway? Hudgens' confession should be enough for the cops to at least bring him in. What's the point of the face-to-face?"

"Hudgens needs it, he says. He's paying me to go with him, so I let him do it his way. I'm working for him, if you can believe that. And if I'm with him, it's easier to keep track of him. I'm taking him in, if nothing else."

"Be careful, Gus. You're playing without looking at your hand. You don't know much about these guys. They could be total whack jobs who won't be fazed by wiping out you and the other three. Alito has a track record for being a pig and a bully. You might end up spilling more blood, maybe your sister gets hurt. You'll wig out for sure if that happens."

"I thought of that and today I talked long and hard at Corrine, but you know how that went. At least they're not going in the restaurant with Hudgens and me."

"That's good."

"We should find Alito at the restaurant. Soapy told Corrine she saw an online review of the place that mentioned the lively, joke-telling manager, Don Allen, who's at the front desk every night it's open. It'll be dinner time, so the place should be busy. Hudgens will call him out, say his peace in front of customers, which should keep Alito and DiNunzio under control. We hope. Meanwhile, Corrine will call 911 to get Colorado Springs cops on the scene. They should be around before Hudgens makes his speech. If it works out, the cops can make sure Alito doesn't disappear. If we don't end up in the Colorado Springs jail, when we get back to Denver, Hudgens finishes this . . . whatever it is, by turning himself in to Denver law."

"Man, that sounds like a lot of 'ifs.' You sure you don't need my help?"

I looked at my old friend with something like affection. The man trembled and limped. He faced a major fight with a serious disease. He'd aged ten years in a few months. Yet he was willing to go along with me, one more time, on another of my crazy and likely dangerous escapades simply because we were friends. And because we were friends, I knew I couldn't put him at risk.

"Thanks, pal. We're good. This thing in Springs is just to help Hudgens deal with his conscience. It'll be over in five minutes. The biggest variable of the plan is that we spook Alito and he manages to skip out and disappear again, this time for good. But, you know what? I don't think I care, as long as Hudgens is locked up and pays for what he did. I'll settle for that. For now. Soapy will find Alito again, if necessary."

Jerome leaned back on his sleek sofa. He clenched and unclenched his hands. He stopped his constantly moving foot.

"You may be right," he said. He didn't look at me. "You and Corrine have this. You don't need my help."

Of course I needed his help. He knew it, I knew it. The trek to Colorado Springs was foolish, unnecessary. Hudgens and I would walk into Alito's home turf, where he was a respected boss, with nothing more than crazy accusations spouted by a homeless addict. The play was ripe for Jerome to be at my side.

"We're cool," I said. "I'll come by tomorrow night and let you know how it shook out."

"Yeah, you do that. Be careful, dude."

He sat on the couch with a book in his lap. Something about living a full life with Parkinson's.

"Any good?" I asked.

He shrugged. "It's a slow read."

I finished my beer and left.

# - Chapter 22 -
## ODYSSEY

I drove up to the curb in front of my house at seven forty-five. I sat in the running pickup, in the dark. I wasn't hungry, and I didn't want to watch TV. I had nothing to do unless I drove the several miles back to my office and put in another three hours of paperwork drudgery. I thought about dropping in on Hudgens at Corrine's house and going over everything again. I didn't move. My mind was stuck in neutral. Whatever had been wrong with me had not cleared up, not completely.

Ah, the life of a private eye—*this* private eye at least. I didn't fool myself. I wasn't finding the cure for cancer. I wasn't busting terrorist cells or carrying kids out of burning apartment buildings. Mostly, I schlepped in the dark for people who wanted to expose the secrets of others or do all they could to keep their own secrets hidden. Often, I was nothing more than a delivery man, or a gofer. I accepted my fate, since most of the negative crap in my life was self-inflicted. I made choices and paid the price for the bad ones, or drifted with the flow of the good ones, rare as those might be.

I believed I was good at my job. I did my best for all my clients, whether they could pay me a twenty-five-grand retainer in cash, or only promise to make it good in the future, sometime, whenever.

I called Ana Domingo, the police community liaison who had sent Hudgens to me. I told myself that she ought to know what had happened with her referral. That was a lie.

She answered quickly, and when I heard her I immediately remembered the nights we'd spent with each other, locked in sexual combat, sweating, groaning, cursing and hollering. She said "hello" with the amber voice that had whispered vulgarities in my ear, that had taunted me with fantasies and that had finally said goodbye and good riddance when she found someone else.

"This is a surprise," she said.

"I thought you should know. Leo Hudgens might resolve his problem tomorrow. Thanks for the referral."

"I'm happy to hear that, Gus. I don't know everything about him, but the way he acted I assumed he needed someone who could be discreet. That's you, for sure."

"Good old discreet Gus. You bet. My lips are sealed."

She laughed.

I waited for her to say goodbye or to keep the conversation going. It was up to her. I'd enjoyed my time with her. I was surprised and, I hated to admit it, hurt when she moved on. She hooked up with a cop from Mexico who helped me work through a situation that came to me by way of Luis Móntez, the now-retired lawyer. Ana had been a part of that case. It didn't end well between us. When I called, I was betting against the odds that it hadn't really ended.

"You sure?" she said, finally. "Nothing I could do to unseal those lips? There was a time when your lips weren't the only part of your body that needed opening up."

Ana was nothing if not a tease. I must've caught her between boyfriends, or all she had planned was a slow TV night.

"Or yours, as I recall." I said it without thinking.

She giggled. "Same old Gus. You talk a good game. You got any follow-through?"

"Can I come over? I can give you more details about Hudgens."

"Fuck that. Come over, but leave Hudgens in your pickup. We have other things to do."

I drove to her apartment.

We spent the first fifteen minutes getting reacquainted. We agreed that nothing much had changed in our lives since the last time we'd been together. We also admitted that our personal lives sucked, and then we promised each other that we were only filling dead space with one night of fun, and nothing more.

I spent the next two hours with no thought of Hudgens or Kino or anything else about my business. I don't know why she wanted me that night, and I didn't care. We had one thing on our minds and we got to it almost immediately. Ana was good, and my mind didn't wander much from the task at hand. The occasional vision of Marita passed through my enriched imagination. Soapy also popped up for a brief but intense minute or two, but Ana always brought me back. We finished, satisfied with ourselves.

We tried to talk, but we knew it was futile, a useless gesture. What we'd had was gone, and the one-night stand, really a two-hour stand, would not bring anything back. Not that a return to old times was what either one of us wanted.

We climbed out of bed and dressed. Ana offered me a drink, and I thought for a minute that I would accept. I didn't, though, and she didn't insist. I kissed her goodnight. It was almost chaste after what we'd been through in her bedroom. We both promised to call.

It felt like a hurried goodbye, and I didn't want to be rude, so I walked slowly to my truck, casual, easy. I turned to wave goodnight. She was gone, her door closed.

Almost at the same instant that I turned the key in the ignition, my phone buzzed. Corrine.

"What's up?" I asked.

"Is Leo with you?"

"Hudgens? No. Why? What's wrong?"

"He didn't show up when he was supposed to. I've been waiting all night. He was scheduled for a shift at the shelter, then we were going to grab a burger and chill out the rest of the night. But he's not here, and I can't get a hold of him."

"Did you try Soapy?"

"Yeah. First thing. She hasn't seen him. He was going to check in with *her*, but that never happened either. She's coming over. I thought I'd ask you, but I knew he wouldn't be with you."

"That son of a bitch."

"Aren't you worried? What if Alito knows what he's up to? What if . . . "

"That's nonsense. How could he? This guy Hudgens realized that it was really happening, and now he's running. He's either on the road or junked up in an alley. I knew that guy was bullshit."

"Calm down, Gus. We gotta look for him. He could be hurt. If he's afraid, we'll have to deal with that, but don't go off half-cocked. Come over here and we'll think this through."

She hung up.

I slammed my palm against the steering wheel. The pickup lurched forward, then died.

"What now," I mumbled.

I turned the key again and the engine growled. It wouldn't catch. I jiggled the key, cussed. I wondered what I'd done to offend the cosmos.

The corner lit up and a pair of headlights glowed in the intersection. The late model sedan, probably a Camry, turned in my direction. I watched it speed towards me. It did not slow down. The headlights went dark, but the car kept coming. It swerved crazily as it bore down on me. I braced for whatever was coming, I gripped the wheel, pressed my legs into the floor. My jaw clenched.

At the last second, the lights went back on and the car angled away from me and my pickup. As it passed, I saw the laughing faces of two young boys and a girl.

I took my time and finally started the pickup. I drove to Corrine's.

ᘒ ᘒ ᘒ

Corrine believed something bad had happened to Hudgens. I was convinced he'd folded like the chickenshit I knew he was. Soapy was neutral. She wasn't invested in him like Corrine or me. She couldn't find him with her computer, which diminished her interest in finding him at all.

We talked for a half-hour before we agreed to search for Hudgens. For Corrine, it meant confirming that the worst had not happened. For me, it meant confirming that he was as worthless as I thought.

The first thing I did was to call Jerome.

"Weren't you just here?" he asked instead of saying hello.

I quickly described the situation.

"You need some help?" he said.

"Right. You have any ideas? The three of us are going to sweep through as many places as we can. You know any to check?"

The phone was silent for a few seconds.

"One," he said. "On the Platte. A tent city, but it's only a few tents. Lot of cardboard and old blankets. Guys who won't stay in a shelter, vets who can't handle people or noise. It's that kind of place. I'll drive over there, give it a look."

It didn't surprise me that Jerome knew all about a homeless camp along the banks of the Platte River.

"You can't go by yourself. I'll go with you."

"No. Stay with Corrine and Soapy. I know a couple of guys who'll go with me."

"Who?"

"You don't know them. They're in one of my PD exercise classes."

That stopped me for a sec. "They can do this?"

"Why not? One guy was a helicopter pilot, military and commercial. The other does martial arts in addition to the PD classes. He's a black belt to the nth degree. Something like that."

"And he's got Parkinson's?"

"All three of us. I figure we can handle one homeless camp. We won't cause any trouble."

"And they're ready tonight?"

"They owe me. I'll call you when we finish with the camp. With a little luck, your guy will be there. Can you send me his photo?"

I could, and I did. I was curious about what favor he'd done for his exercise buddies, but that had to wait.

Corrine, Soapy and I squeezed into my pickup and started our odyssey through places that we knew only because we drove by them at rush hour and saw the lines of men, women and children waiting for a meal with a prayer, or a dry mattress, or a bottle of water and a minute of peace.

We looked for him at the shelter where he volunteered. Nothing. We checked the Rescue Mission kitchen. *Nada.* We talked to people gathered at the offices of the Coalition for the Homeless, and on the littered sidewalks along Lawrence Street and Twentieth Avenue. No sign of Leo Hudgens. We visited alleys, bridges along bike paths, park benches. We talked with panhandlers holding cardboard signs at major intersections. Most of the time we were greeted with blank, even hostile stares. No one had seen him, no one admitted they knew him. We asked for him at emergency rooms of the midtown hospitals and waiting rooms of urgent care centers. Our last stop was the city jail. Another blank.

The guy had disappeared into the gray world of the dispossessed, a world that none of us knew anything about, and that seemed as strange as if we'd crashed onto a lost and unforgiving alternate planet.

We gave up looking for him by midnight.

We were exhausted, but Soapy and Corrine said they were hungry. I parked the truck at the all-night diner at the intersection of Colfax and Speer.

Jerome called as I slammed the pickup's door shut.

"Anything?" I asked.

"Lots of stuff, but not your guy. Sorry. One old timer admitted knowing him, but said it'd been years since he'd seen him. I think he was feeding us a line. A woman said she could take us to him if we bought her a bottle of whiskey. I figured that was a dead end."

"Thanks anyway, Jerome. And thank your friends."

"I will, and so will you, soon. You owe them a drink or two, probably some happy hour apps, too."

"Goes without saying. Glad nothing went haywire out there."

"Yeah, but there's a story. I'll save it for happy hour."

The diner was busy with potheads and drunks, and we waited ten minutes until one of the tables was wiped clean. Soapy ordered pancakes, Corrine asked for a salad, and I just wanted coffee.

"He's gone," Corrine said. "He must have left town earlier today, before he was supposed to talk with Soapy. Probably hitchhiked and by now could be in New Mexico."

"Or Grand Junction, maybe Wyoming," Soapy said.

"We could go to Colorado Springs," Corrine said. "Tomorrow, maybe he'll . . . "

"You're not serious," I said. "He's not going to be there. He's taken off, and we'll be better off if we forget him. I'm sorry I got you two involved. Sorry I introduced you to Leo Hudgens. I've wasted your time for a guy who didn't deserve it."

We talked a few minutes more about Hudgens and the places we'd seen that night. I cursed more than talked. Then the food and drinks arrived, and we quit talking. By the time we left the restaurant, Corrine and Soapy were in better moods. Soapy tried to tell a joke she'd heard in one of her classes, but she botched the punch line, and we laughed at *her* instead. I paid the bill with one of the wrinkled and stained fifty dollar bills that Hudgens had given me as a deposit for "future services."

"At least his body didn't turn up," Corrine said when I dropped her off at her house.

"That's something, I guess," Soapy said as she also climbed down from my truck.

I said goodnight and left it at that.

Later, when I sat in the darkness of my house, nursing a beer, I imagined Hudgens passed out on dope, his clean clothes and barbered hair stained with mud and vomit. I wanted to think the worst about him. He'd betrayed Corrine and Soapy, and for that I wanted him to suffer. I kept myself off that short list, since I'd never believed he would follow through on his fantasy of publicly humiliating Dominick Alito, or his Hollywood ending of heroically facing the music by turning himself in to the police. I remembered the stench he left in my office the first time I met him, and that was how I chose to think of him.

I recalled the ragged children we'd encountered in our search. Young but already losing hope with every cold day without a warm meal or bed. Again, I saw the men and women who were crippled by booze or drugs or their own minds and who lived with constant desperation, or the veterans wounded first in their service and then again by their country's neglect. I felt the anger and fear and fatigue, and it made me hate Hudgens more. He had a chance to rise above it all, although it meant going to prison. Somehow, I concluded he owed that to the people waiting in the food lines and sprawled on the sidewalks. Instead, he'd thrown it away without even bothering to show up.

I drank several beers, one after the other, without tasting them. I fell asleep in the recliner, my television on without sound, my brain turned off, the only noise a low-level hum of resignation that vibrated through my core.

# - Chapter 23 -
## NEVER ON SUNDAY

A few weeks later, on a Sunday, I drove the several miles to my office to retrieve the newspaper and, along the way, to buy a latte from Jerome at his coffee shop.

Jerome wasn't in. I ordered the coffee to go.

I read the newspaper at my desk. While I read, my used and banged-up radio was tuned to Pocho Joe's show, La Raza Rocks. The mix of Chicano soul, oldies and new Latino rock reminded me of my father's musical tastes. He would've been a big fan of Pocho's, like I was.

I didn't intend to work. "Never on Sunday," I told myself.

The start of baseball season was less than a week away, which meant that on Friday night a snowstorm blew across the state, dropped the temperature into single digits and iced the freeways. I-70 westbound was closed at Georgetown; eastbound was locked down at Limon. I shoveled my way out of my house Saturday morning, and I couldn't warm up my feet that night until I put on two pairs of socks and covered them with a blanket as I watched TV.

Sunday morning was a different story all-together. The sun turned the piled and drifted snow into brilliant white flashes. The temp climbed into the forties, melted snow flowed in the gutters, and it almost felt like spring.

After all the excitement of Cuba, and the wear-and-tear on my delicate psyche from the Hudgens episode, the past weeks of work were a vacation: I finished off several jobs that had simmered while I was gone, I let attorneys and potential clients know I was back, cleaned up the office, resumed my exercise routine and finally slept better. I ate more food and basically put to rest the vague shadows that'd haunted me. I thought I'd turned a corner.

I planned to do the crossword after I caught up on the latest rumors from Spring training. I couldn't help myself: the Rockies had become tabloid fodder. Several stories in March focused on the antics of Rockies players. The team was more entertaining than any of the Mexican soap operas Corrine watched with religious regularity.

A backup catcher was stopped for running a red light in Phoenix. The city police arrested him for drunk driving. His passenger, a stripper whose stage name was Champagne Sunset, posted his bail. The next news story about the catcher confirmed that his wife filed for divorce—the stripper was her sister.

One of the middle relievers tripped on his infant son's scooter. He broke the index finger of his throwing hand and was expected to miss the first six weeks of the season. Twitter exploded with speculation that the pitcher was addicted to painkillers from a previous injury and he was high when he fell, but that's as far as that went.

Three days after that episode, the Rockies camp was shaken with an announcement from the Commissioner's Office. The all-star second baseman, a young Texas kid raised near the El Paso border and a finalist for last year's Rookie of the Year Award, was suspended indefinitely. Turned out his mother brought him to the States from Mexico when he was an infant. The kid had always assumed he was a citizen of the United States. One of the owners of the rival San Diego Padres challenged that assumption, and now everyone scrambled to figure out the complicated immigration status of the young man and whether he could legally play baseball in the United States.

"All I want to do is play ball," he said to the *Post* reporter. "I love my country: the United States."

There were others, but the story that popped up repeatedly described, in agonizing statistical detail, the horrific spring Joaquín Machaco was enduring. The exhibition games were nightmares, the first few games of the new season not much better.

He couldn't buy a hit. He made several errors in his usual position at center field, and there was talk that the manager might try him at first base, more as a wake-up call than as a serious look at a new position for Kino. At times he appeared lost, especially on the rare occasions when he got on base. More than one ESPN commentator pointed out that the Rockies had another potential superstar center fielder waiting in the wings, and that maybe it was time to give the minor-leaguer a chance to show his stuff. It was so bad that the sports writers and analysts simply referred to "The Slump," and everyone knew they were reporting on Kino Machaco.

I wondered if there was more to Kino's slump than simply a slow start. Had the recent events in Cuba affected him more than anyone realized? As if he was listening to my wandering thoughts, I got a call from one of the few people in the world who might be able to answer my question.

"Gus? This is Ben Sardo. Remember me?"

"Kino's agent. Sure. What you up to?"

The home opener for the Rockies was that week. The city eagerly awaited the party around the stadium in lower downtown Denver that started off each season since the team played its first home game back in 1993. This opening day promised to be extra special because of the team's World Series appearance the year before. Trophies would be handed out and speeches made about the great year the team had had. The fans would be eager to watch the first home game of a season that they expected to finish with a follow-up Series that, this year, the Rockies would win. I assumed Sardo was in town for the game, but I had no idea why he'd call me.

"I got good news. From Kino. He wants to give you tickets to opening day. Kind of a bonus for all your hard work, all the trouble you went through for him and his family. How many you want? These are good seats, Gus. VIP, top of the line. You can have a party. No one will bother you."

"He doesn't have to do that."

"It's already done. How many?"

I quickly calculated whether any of my sisters or friends would go to Coors Field with me. Why not? Opening day was all about fun in the sun and the National Pastime, and it was Denver's favorite sports day, when the Broncos weren't in the Super Bowl, or the Avalanche wasn't playing for the Stanley Cup, or the Nuggets . . .

"Six. I'll take six."

I knew at least five people who would go to a game with me, didn't I?

The irony was obvious. Gus Corral, a guy from the old Northside streets, an ex-con with a mistake-riddled history, would bump elbows with the rich and famous, the movers and the shakers. The power brokers of Colorado's booming economy and ravenous growth could be behind me in the beer line. I might sit next to one of the state's new marijuana moguls, who couldn't spend his millions fast enough; or the developer who'd stripped my neighborhood of its history, culture and personality; or the politician who had the president's private line in his contacts list. If I'd thought too hard about it, I might've gotten dizzy, even sick.

"They're yours, Gus. Gonna be a great game. The Dodgers will be in town, you know that, right?"

"Sure."

"The tickets will be under your name at Will Call. See you then."

The guy was in a perpetual rush.

"Before you go, how's Kino doing? He okay? From what I've read, he's still not hitting."

He paused. He must've bit his lip. "Yeah, he's good. Don't believe what you read about him. He comes alive when the real season starts, usually a few weeks into it. Always been that way. I won't be surprised if he busts out for the home opener. We've seen this before."

He was upbeat, confident, covering his client's back.

"Yeah, okay. I guess. But it sounds different from past seasons. Hope he's not hurt."

"Don't worry about Kino Machaco."

The slight edge that creeped into his voice told me he was tired of answering questions about the dependability of his biggest meal ticket. How many times would he have to defend Kino and explain The Slump?

"You and everyone else are gonna see some amazing baseball from Kino this year. There's no doubt in my mind."

"I'm sure you're right."

"You took a load off his mind with the work you did in Cuba. So, it's all good, no worry."

"Glad to hear that. I'd still like to meet with him. That possible? We never talked when I got back from Cuba. He must've heard all about the trip from Alberto and Lourdes, but I would like to talk with him, if it can be arranged. Share thoughts about Cuba."

"This is a crazy week, you realize that, right?"

"Five minutes. I really appreciate that he came to me." *Although the trip almost killed me*, I thought. "I want to tell him that myself."

"The team's out of town. They opened in San Francisco."

"They have to be here Friday for the home opener."

"It'll be tight."

I could almost see him looking at the calendar on his cell while he talked to me.

"Thursday's their travel day. That evening, the night before the game, he's scheduled for an appearance at the fan appreciation party in the big tent outside the stadium. He'll sign autographs and pose for photographs with fans. When he's done there, he'll be in my office for about an hour, around eight o'clock. We have to dot i's and cross t's. If it's important, you could talk to him then. Five minutes, Gus. That's all."

"I'll be there and gone before you know it. What's the address?"

"It's my new office in Denver. I think you'll like it."

He gave me a downtown Seventeenth Street address in one of the high rises that stood out in photographs of Denver's skyline. It might as well have been in another country. Although I could see the top of his building through the grimy window of my office, in truth, Sardo operated in a different world. I had no doubt I'd be impressed with his office.

After the call I thought about why I wanted to talk with Kino. I'd been paid, the job was over. The money was back in whatever account he decided on, and the threat to Alberto was dead, really dead. No good reason to meet with the super jock, unless I'd suddenly become a fan and wanted his autograph on a baseball. That wasn't it. I told myself it was something I needed to do, even if I didn't understand why. What I did understand was that there were unanswered questions lingering, fluttering, nagging. Details to be taken care of and accounted for. Like Sardo said, dotting i's and crossing t's.

Without thinking about it, I went through a half-dozen files. Gus Corral, private eye, was on the case. Or, rather, counting hours on a variety of sexy assignments: serving subpoenas, following wayward husbands and wives, digging into personal and private matters that should have stayed personal and private. I finished the reports, memos, affidavits and invoices I needed to close out the accounts and mail my final bill. When I looked up from the desk and realized I was clearing it, I stopped. What happened to "Never on Sunday"?

I texted Maxine, my younger sister. Was she interested in opening day? I had tickets. She and Sandra could have a pair, if she wanted them. She responded almost immediately with emojis of balloons, fireworks, a unicorn, a baseball bat and a beer mug. I took all that as a yes. I texted back that she should meet me at Will Call at the stadium an hour before the game. She sent an animated pair of ruby red lips, blowing a kiss.

Maxine loved baseball. She'd played the game as a kid and developed a reputation as a tough little infielder. No one slid into her at third unless they were willing to risk a bruised rib from a hard tag or a bloodied nose from a knee blocking the bag. And she could hit, not for power necessarily but for a timely single to bring in the tying run, or a double when she put everything she had into her swing and connected.

Maxine studied baseball and baseball history. Her senior year in high school she sought out an elderly great aunt who lived in the small town of Florence because of our mother's stories about the aunt's baseball days as a young girl. The aunt grew up in the mining town of Chandler, a company town that died when the mine played out. A few years before Chandler became a ghost town, one of the miners organized an all-girl softball team that played games throughout Southern Colorado—Pueblo, Cañon City, Penrose, Westcliffe, Beulah and others. The coal miners' daughters were Mexicans, Italians, Eastern Europeans. According to the aunt, the team was *excelente*, winners. The woman's stories amazed Maxine.

"In those days," she told me when she returned to Denver, "you could still find signs in restaurants that said, 'No dogs or Mexicans.' This was in the forties. Can you imagine what it must've been like? But this miner, their coach, a Mexican himself, did all he could for the girls of the mining camp. He found rides for them to games, dug up mitts, bats and balls . . . and he coached them at night after his shift in the mine. It's a great piece of Colorado history, and Aunt Eladia couldn't stop talking about playing baseball with the tough Chandler girls. She may not remember what she had for breakfast, but she remembers playing baseball in Chandler."

For a guy who wasn't much of a sports fan, I looked forward to enjoying the game with Max and Sandra. We'd drink beer and talk about her band, married life and the latest Corrine squabble. Most important, she could explain that there really was something going on when it looked like everyone on the field, including the umpires, were standing around, playing with their mitts, spitting or grabbing their crotches.

I made one more call.

Jerome hesitated when I asked him if he wanted the remaining tickets for himself and the guys who'd joined in the search for Leo Hudgens.

"We have a balance class on Friday. Hate to miss it."

He finally accepted when I said he could give the tickets to anyone if he couldn't make it.

I caught myself stealing glances at files and some of my notes. I decided I should leave and do something that involved sunshine and brisk air.

I was about to lock up when someone knocked on the door. I opened it and recognized the collection agency receptionist from down the hall. She wore skinny jeans and a loose sweatshirt, a big difference from her usual uptight office-serious look.

"I thought I saw you come in," she said. "I was glad. I hate being in this place by myself. It's creepy."

Another first: she talked to me. Normally, she avoided me like the building mice ignored the janitor's cat. She always seemed to be typing demand letters, filing papers or answering the telephone, and certainly without any time for small talk with me.

"You're working today?"

"Finishing a few things. We have so much work. Feels like nobody pays their bills."

"I can sympathize with that. What can I do for you?"

She handed me a collection of envelopes, large and small, wrapped with a rubber band.

"That crazy postman left all your mail with the temp they had in here Friday. I didn't make it in because of the snow. Damn car wouldn't start. Not sure why he gave us your mail. By chance, did you get any of ours?"

"I don't think so, but let me check. Come in."

She walked in and looked around the office with an expression I couldn't decipher. It might have been as innocent as "So this is what a private eye's office looks like." But probably not.

I went through the mail on my desk. No envelopes addressed to the New Age Collection and Debt Management Service.

"Sorry, nothing for you guys."

"Okay. I was hoping you'd say that. Like I said, we've already got too much work."

She made it as far as the door, then turned around.

"My name's Lorraine. Lorraine Winston."

"Nice to meet you, Lorraine. I'm Gus…"

"Gus Corral," she said. "I know."

She strolled down the hallway. She looked back one more time, then entered her office.

Any other day I might've followed her and asked if she wanted to take a break, get some coffee, maybe a beer. But one of the letters in the bunch she gave me grabbed my complete attention. It was covered with unusual stamps and Spanish words. The return address was for Lourdes Rivera of La Habana, Cuba.

*Querido Agustín—Gus,*

*This letter must be a surprise. I hope you are doing well, especially after all the trouble we ran into here in Cuba. If you ever return, and I hope you do, I promise I will show you the true heart of Cuba—the music, art and beauty of the people, the things we had no time for when you were here.*

*Professor Raúl Suárez of the Language Institute is writing this in English for me, to make sure you can read what I want to say. He is a trusted old friend. Esteban Sánchez was his brother-in-law. I am sure you remember Esteban.*

*I write to tell you what has happened since you returned to your home. I think you have a right to know.*

*The official version, from the policeman, Federico Solís, is that the two criminals, Eduarda Ventura and Mario Faustino, planned to steal the money that was to be paid to Miguel. You must know by now they were killed by the police, and for Federico and the Havana police, that is the end of the matter. No one else has been arrested, and since the money was never actually stolen, the government officials are agreed that is the end. Havana is once again considered safe for businesses and tourists. The shootings and killings have been labeled as "aberrations" committed by a small terrorist element of anti-revolutionaries that have been eliminated.*

*That is supposed to make us feel secure.*

I have started to rebuild the beach house. I stay in an apartment in the city, but I miss the beautiful evenings by the shore and the quiet mornings I once took for granted. It will be several months, however, before my home will be ready. The construction and planning require all my attention, but they help to keep my mind off the terrible things that happened because of Alberto's money. I can only hope that Alberto has finally learned something, and that he never puts himself or Kino, or me, in such a situation again.

Perhaps the biggest surprise for you, and you might not believe me, is that Marita and I have drawn closer together. We did have Miguel in common. That may sound strange to you, but I am not ashamed to admit that I loved him at one time, and it is obvious that Marí still does. But her relationship with Miguel was very complicated, and when he was killed, she was planning to leave him. His death caused her much guilt and grief, and only recently has she become more like her old self.

Marí feels so much better that she is visiting relatives in Miami. She left this morning and plans to be in the United States for a month. From my past experiences with my letters to Joaquín and Alberto, you could receive this letter in Denver three weeks or a month after I mail it. She may be back here by the time you read this.

I think that is everything. Joaquín informed me that he is eager for the new season to begin, and, as always, all eyes in Cuba will be on him, although we are careful about expressing too much admiration for such a well-known defector. I wish him well. Will you have a chance to watch him play?

A thousand gratitudes for everything. I am happy I met you. Perhaps we will meet again one day.

Hugs and affection,
Lourdes

I read the letter twice. Lourdes had made me feel better. I had a certain *cariño* for the woman. She had affected me with her intelligence and honesty.

Lourdes was an incredibly strong person. I, too, was happy we had met, regardless of the circumstances. She had more going for her than she let on, that was apparent. She was not a simple bureaucrat, as she tried to convince me when I recuperated at her beach house. Her influence, connections and wealth meant she was someone important in the Cuban social order, most likely to the Cuban government. I hoped for her sake that Havana was as safe and secure as the propagandists promised, and that life would return to normal for her, whatever that truly meant on her island of secrets.

I left the office with the letter in my hands. Lorraine was not at her desk, so I spent the rest of that beautiful Sunday walking and running in the sunshine, breathing the crisp air and letting my body and mind heal in the realization that life was good, or bearable at least for the time being.

# – Chapter 24 –
## STORMY MONDAY

The weather hopped on a roller coaster fueled by global warming, and Monday landed gray and cold. On again-off again snow mixed with rain as if a solid decision about the season had not been made. One day sunshine, next day sleet, then sunshine. The nine o'clock morning rush-hour drive into SoBo and my office was slow and frustrating. Nothing new.

I steered around impatient drivers who somehow believed that their rides were ice-proof, transplants who acted as though they'd never seen snow and natives who never learned how to drive as defensively as I had. The Wild West survived on Colorado's packed freeways and in Denver's congested rush hours, more so when snow fell. In my pickup, I often felt separate from the craziness. Until someone tapped my rear end and then flipped me off, or went speeding by, spraying slush in a lane that didn't exist.

The baseball game on Friday would most likely begin with fans wearing shorts and sunscreen. By the seventh inning we'd be in coats, even a few parkas. April baseball in Colorado could be a challenge, especially for someone like me who could take it or leave it.

I played with the idea that I'd accept Lourdes' offer and return to Cuba, maybe in the fall. Kino's check sat safely in my office account, and I still had a few hundred left of the upfront expense money. I could pay rent for a couple of months, get new tires for the pickup and look for a suit that would enhance my P.I. image but not be too out of place in the dark and grimy halls of the Lewis Building. Something that might impress Lorraine Winston, a nice hat, maybe a fedora. And then a visit to Lourdes and Havana. Would Lorraine want to join me?

I was way ahead of myself, but it didn't matter. I'd talked with Lorraine once. We'd made a connection, slim but with potential, and I thought she was interested. I was certainly interested in her. Aloof and serious women held a certain attraction for this Northside homeboy, although I'd rarely cracked the mystery of an intriguing smile or fulfilled the promise of a sweet laugh. If I was going to dream, make it big. Someone said that once, but I didn't remember who.

The radio in my pickup was a good one, and I often listened to oldies or country music as I drove. That morning the dial was on the news station. I left it there, in case the flurry turned into a full-frontal storm that the weather crew somehow missed. Hey, it'd happened from time to time.

Maybe the president would provide more laughs. One thing about that guy, he was great for gallows humor, even though he didn't know what that meant.

But the main story was about another shooting on I-25. That morning, around seven, before the storm hit, the I-25 shooter had killed a motorist in a snarl of traffic at the Briargate Street entrance to the freeway in far north Colorado Springs. The police were concerned that the shooter had escalated his attacks. A high-powered rifle was the killing weapon, rather than a .22 handgun. The motorist was shot as he waited to merge onto the highway, not when he was already on it. This was no drive-by. It appeared the shooter had set up a hidden outpost, more like a hunting blind, on a short rise about a hundred yards from the freeway. The shooter had chosen the perfect spot for his killing nest. It was protected from the back by a noise-deflecting wall and from the front by bushes and boulders. He could pick off drivers at will as they waited in traffic. The police were surprised that only one commuter had been shot.

"There were dozens of drivers and passengers sitting at that entrance," the police spokesman said. "He must have been scared away by something after his first shot. It could have been a massacre."

One more threat to worry about.

The news story finished with the usual notice. "Identity of the victim has been withheld pending notification of family and next-of-kin."

I blanked out the rest of the news and focused on staying on the street. The tires of the pickup were worn, almost bald, and I had little to no traction on ice. I almost lost control a couple of times. Whatever ambition I'd started the day with had been knocked out of me by the time I finally pulled into my parking space.

Lorraine sat at her desk when I walked by. I stomped snow and mud off my boots and shook out my coat. She heard me and looked up.

"You're late," she said. She wasn't particularly happy to see me.

"I almost wrecked my truck," I said. "It's bad out there."

"You should take the bus, like me."

"That's a thought," I answered.

I was about to ask her about her Sunday night when she blurted out, "There's a girl waiting for you. She had a key, so I guess it's okay that she's there." Lorraine acted hurt about something, but there was no good reason.

*Jesus,* I said to myself. *Now what?*

"Uh, thanks," I mumbled.

Soapy had made herself at home in my office. She had papers arranged across my desk and on the chairs. Her laptop was plugged in and running a spreadsheet. She stared intently at a piece of paper that she held close to her face.

"What is all this?" I asked.

"You asked me to look at the ballplayer's finances, and the businesses he shares with his brother. You remember that, right?"

"Sure. But that was before I went to Cuba, for background on what I was getting into. I thought you already gave me what you had. And anyway, that job is finished."

"You never said to quit looking, so I've been at it. You want me to stop, I will, but there are a few interesting things that you should probably know."

The thing about Soapy that I often forgot was that she was still a young person, just a few years past being called a child. Her self-confidence, cockiness really, around computers and all other things techie made her appear older than she was. But occasionally she didn't have enough experience to understand the big picture. She sometimes faltered without direct, clear and watchful supervision. That was one reason she kept digging into the financial life of Kino long after I needed such information.

"I don't know if I can pay for this," I said. "Damn, how many hours you put in?"

"I haven't run totals yet, but don't sweat it, Sherlock."

"You been talking to Jerome?"

"Your friend? Why do you ask that?"

"Nevermind. Like I said, what's this gonna cost me?"

"You need to know this stuff. I think you'll like it."

"I'll like it?"

"Well, at least you'll be glad you got it."

She was right. Well, maybe not "glad" exactly. The information didn't make me happy, but it went a long way to shedding light on the darker corners of the Cuban trip. I worked out a payment plan with Soapy—it seemed only right—and together we wrote up a report that I would use when I met with Kino in Ben Sardo's office. As she was leaving, I gave her a big hug. That's when Lorraine walked out of her office and saw Soapy and me in an embrace. Lorraine hustled down the hallway without a word. Soapy followed her, whistling a nonsensical melody that must've made sense to a mind that could create computer games from scratch and uncover encrypted secrets never meant for exposure to light.

Mondays can be hard in any business. They're always hard in mine—that's a sure bet. Shit often happens on weekends. Monday mornings are hell on doctors, teachers, lawyers and private eyes.

I had to come to grips with the fact that I, and I alone, was totally responsible for the success or failure of my business. If I worked long hours, brought in new business every week and by myself accomplished what three other investigators could do, I might break even at the end of the year, after my big payday from Kino Machaco ran out. It would be close.

After Soapy left, my phone wouldn't quit ringing. A trio of rude lawyers wanted to know why I hadn't filed my proofs of service that they needed for their subpoenas, court complaints and discovery requests. A camera shop wanted to know when I would pick up the black-and-whites they'd developed on a rush basis, which I'd forgotten about. The bill was way past due. One client wanted a refund because she and her husband had reconciled and so it didn't matter anymore that he'd cheated on her. Another fired me because the lie detector test I'd administered to his ex-business partner was ambiguous about the partner's honesty, a risk I warned him about the first day he talked to me. And on and on.

Lorraine didn't make it any easier. I noticed her occasionally, usually when I walked past the collection agency's door while she sat at the receptionist's desk. Most often, all I caught was a glimpse of her profile, but that day it felt like she was everywhere I looked: down the hall, in the conference room, on her way to the restroom, downstairs on break. I tried to start a conversation, but she put me off with weak excuses about her need to get back to work. I hardly knew the woman and she was already giving me the brush-off. I finally decided that the mental wear-and-tear wasn't worth it. If I'd done something offensive, I would've apologized, but I couldn't come up with anything other than a few impure thoughts I'd had about her. She couldn't know about *those*, right? They were only venial sins anyway.

I finished the day doing leg work. One of my clients owned a grocery store in the Globeville neighborhood. He was about ready to throw in the towel, file bankruptcy and cut his losses. But before he pulled the plug, he wanted to make sure there weren't any plans to develop the low-income neighborhood where he did business.

This was a new trend in Denver. The hell-bent gentrification of several areas of the city had changed the character of many neighborhoods. Poor businessmen suddenly owned valuable real estate. If their timing was right, they could cash in by selling to a marijuana company or a condo designer or a restaurant chain. If the timing was off, they'd sell for less than fifty cents on the ultimate dollar. My guy wanted me to check corporate filings, property sales in his community, secretary of state registrations and so on. I might have been able to do what he wanted by computer, but I had to get away from the buzzing phone and Lorraine's stonewalling. I trooped downtown and pestered clerks and secretaries until the relevant government offices closed and I was told to leave.

Then I went home, had a Swanson's Salisbury Steak frozen dinner, watched a rerun of *Law & Order* and again slept on the recliner in my living room.

# - Chapter 25 -
## RUBY TUESDAY

Marita Valdés wore a ruby red ski jacket with fur lining. Her lipstick matched her jacket, which matched her western boots. Unlike the last time I'd seen her, she did not have red eyes. She smiled when I answered the knock on my front door. It took me a second, but eventually I smiled back at her. It was six-thirty in the morning. A weird morning.

As if she had planned the coordination, the eastern sky glowed with a warm reddish tint. The snow and rain were gone but the air was frigid. When I opened the door, my face felt like it'd been slapped by a cold and icy rag.

I was dressed in the sweat pants and sweatshirt I'd slept in. The clothes I'd worn on Monday were piled on the kitchen floor. I hadn't showered or shaved.

And yet, she didn't seem disappointed.

"Agustín!" she said, still smiling.

She stepped into my house, hugged me and kissed my cheek. Her subtle perfume surrounded me. I remembered the first time I'd seen her, in Cuba, and the same sensation crept up my spine. Her beauty had stopped me in my tracks. Although Lourdes and I were paying off a Cuban sleaze ball, and bullets flew within minutes of meeting Hoochie and Marita, her image stayed with me almost as long as the memories of the dying Hoochie and the hitman's blood on the restaurant stairs.

That image of Marita gradually faded away, replaced with the sad and exhausted woman who tried to drown herself in the Bay of Pigs. She'd lost her glimmer and poise. That's how I saw her when I told my Cuban story to Jerome and my sisters. The woman at my front door on that moody Tuesday morning, though, was not the same person. Beautiful Marita was back.

"Come in," I said, resigned to my current state of appearance.

She surveyed the house and her face didn't give her away. The living room was furnished with an old couch, torn recliner, a television screen on the wall and not much else. Water stains spotted the ceiling. The kitchen was a disaster. Towels and underwear sat folded on a night stand next to the bathroom door. She must've thought that something was seriously wrong with me. How could a North American *yanqui* live in such conditions?

I was acutely aware of my bare feet and the sleep in my eyes. I started to stammer small talk, when she shook her head.

"I am sorry to interrupt," she said. "I owe you an explanation. On impulse, I caught an overnight flight from Miami. I had planned to see Joaquín and Alberto, but they are out of town. That was always the idea, but I am a few days early. We never set an exact date. I want to see the mountains and your beautiful city. Yesterday, before my flight, I spoke with Joaquín's agent, *el señor* Sardo. He's the one who gave me your address, for your office, too. But I think I made a mistake. You don't look happy to see me. Perhaps it's too early? I should have waited to meet you at your office. And of course, I should have called first. I'm sorry. I'll leave. My driver can take me to the hotel."

I looked out on the street and saw a parked Infiniti luxury sedan. A tall bearded man leaned against the car. He smoked a cigar.

"You're here now," I said. I doubted that she'd made a mistake. "It's good to see you. I'm half asleep, that's all. Why wouldn't I be happy to see you? After all we've been through together? Would you like coffee? Tea? I don't have much for breakfast."

"Coffee would be good. But don't go to any trouble."

Good thing she chose coffee. I didn't have any tea, but I did have a fancy espresso maker that Jerome had given me as a housewarming gift. It was an extra machine delivered to his shop by mistake. I rarely used it, since it was a bear to clean, but I'd make an exception for Marita.

I messed with the coffee machine for about ten minutes. The delay helped me get my thoughts together. When the machine started making noise, I put bread in my toaster, then found peanut butter and grape jelly. I made two cups of the strong coffee, put everything on a tray and carried it to the table. Marita sat quietly, watching me. She'd draped her jacket across the back of her chair. Under the jacket she wore a multicolored western shirt with pearl snaps. We hadn't said another word.

"Your driver want something, some coffee maybe?"

She shook her head. "No. Antonio's fine. He waits for me all the time."

"He's with you? From Cuba?"

"Of course. I'd never travel in this country on my own, it's not safe. Too many guns."

I looked out the window again. Antonio hadn't moved. He still smoked a cigar.

She tried to drink the coffee but stopped almost immediately. "*¿Azúcar, por favor?* You wouldn't have any sugar, would you?"

I hunted down the half-dozen packets of sugar I'd saved from my last trip to Jerome's shop. She opened each one and emptied them into her cup—that Cuban sweet tooth. She stirred the coffee and sipped. A smile parted her red lips.

"Why are you here?" I asked. "What can I do for you?"

"I told you. I have business with Joaquín and Alberto."

"That may be, but why are you here, in my house? You don't have any business with me. Not that I know of." The words came out harsher than I intended.

"I thought we were friends, Gus. Am I wrong?"

"We know one another, and we went through hard events in Cuba. I'm willing to say that makes us more than strangers. Not sure about friends, though. You and your husband were in conflict with my clients, remember?"

"And now I am friends, true friends, with Lourdes. Whatever animosity we had, it's gone. We talk every day. If she can forgive me, why can't you?"

"You want my forgiveness? I don't think there is anything for me to forgive you for." I paused.

She pushed away the toast and the coffee.

"But if Lourdes has no resentment against you, then neither do I."

"Thank you, Gus."

She would not look at me. I continued to stare at her red lips. At last she raised her eyes.

"That night," she said, "in Trinidad . . . I was drunk, out of my mind. I'd just lost Miguel. I didn't know what I was doing."

"Don't worry about that."

"You could have taken advantage. You didn't. I should thank you for that."

"As I said, don't worry about that."

"*Eres un caballero.* Thank you."

My brain tried hard to work its way around what was happening. Had Marita really come all the way from Cuba to tell me that she embarrassed herself and to express gratitude for me not acting like my usual asshole self? Was she just killing time until she could meet with the Machaco brothers?

Her cell phone buzzed. She dug it out of a pocket of the ski jacket and checked the phone's screen.

"Señor Sardo. Buenos días. What can I do for you?"

She listened for several seconds. She nodded her head and muttered "Sí, sí," several times. At one point she looked at me and said, "Of course." She hung up.

"That was Joaquín's agent. You know him, right? He says that since you also want to talk with Joaquín, we should all meet in the agent's office. *Jueves por la noche.*"

"Thursday night? You'll be there, too, huh?"

"It appears so. That means I'll have a few days to see your beautiful Denver. I only hope it warms up."

"It will," I said. "I promise." Suddenly I was Stormy Corral, crack weather person.

We talked for several more minutes about Cuba, Lourdes and life after Hoochie. One thing I learned was that she owned the restaurant on her own now, and although it'd been only a few weeks, she complained that the work load was heavy and guessed that she would eventually sell the business.

"As much as any business can be bought or sold in Cuba," she said.

She kissed me goodbye, on the cheek again, and promised to see me at the agent's office later in the week. She suggested we have lunch or dinner before the meeting, but she didn't sound that sincere, so I didn't follow her lead. We made no additional plans.

She wiggled into her jacket, checked her hair and make-up in a pocket mirror and then she was gone.

Her lilac scent remained. I remembered it mixed with the smell of gunshots and blood in Cuba, the night her husband died at her feet. Until then, I'd never thought of lilacs as flowers of death.

꙳ ꙳ ꙳

I recovered from the morning surprise as best I could. Tuesday meant working out at the Planet Fitness near my house before I drove into the city. I exercised several muscles, joints and tendons for almost ninety minutes. Then I felt ready for the office and any other unexpected guests the day might bring. Couldn't have been more wrong if I'd tried.

I decided on my way in that I should deal with Lorraine. Something had happened between us, but I didn't know what. I had to clear the air if I hoped to have at least a shot with her.

I liked what I'd seen, so far. She had a sense of humor. She was perky, but not in an annoying way. I thought I'd ask about getting together for a drink after work, then play it by ear. I didn't know why she'd cold-shouldered me yesterday, but I could work through that. There was no rush, no need to hurry. Let's just see where this goes, I thought.

The door to the collection agency was shut when I walked past it. I hesitated, then I kept on to my office. Maybe later.

Turned out I didn't have to wait. The office door was unlocked. When I pushed it open completely, Lorraine Winston sat in one of my office chairs. Her legs were crossed, and her fingers tapped the chair's arm. It was a day full of surprising women, and the morning had barely started.

"What the hell, Lorraine?"

"I have keys to the offices. We've been here forever, so Sam sometimes asks us to help with management things, like getting into locked offices."

She spoke with a forced reserve. She was tight, ready to burst.

"That's great, but what do you want? That's really my question."

I made my way around her, stood a little off to her side.

"I want to know what you're up to," she said. "Who do you think you are? You can't treat me like this." Her words flew out of her mouth.

I braced myself. "Treat you like what? I have no idea what you are talking about."

She went limp in the chair. Her legs straightened, and she looked like a plastic doll tossed in a corner.

"I thought you were different," she said. Her voice gradually rose in volume. "You're like all the rest. Once you get what you want, you move on like I'm a useless toy." She stopped for a heartbeat. "I'm nobody's toy."

I gave her the benefit of my doubt and assumed she was kidding around, playing an elaborate joke on me, so I laughed.

She jumped to her feet and pounded my chest with her fist. "You son of a bitch!" she shouted. "Don't you dare laugh at me!" She continued to hit me.

I grabbed her wrists and held them at her sides. "Calm down. Lorraine, whatever I did, I'm sorry."

She squirmed and jerked and twisted as she tried to free herself. I worried that someone would hear her and jump to the wrong conclusion about what was happening between the Chicano ex-con and the petite white secretary.

"Get a hold of yourself. There's nothing wrong."

She hollered again, screamed, really. "You bastard! You ugly Mexican! You perverted pig! Get your filthy hands off me!"

Ugly?

I gave serious consideration to slapping her. That wouldn't help. Instead, I kept her at bay the best I could.

I stared at her face. It twisted into a mask of hate and panic. Spit dribbled from her lips. She continued to make loud noises. No more words, only grunts, growls and an ugly squeaking sound that came from the back of her throat.

I felt, more than saw, that a door in the hallway opened. Then another. I looked over Lorraine's shoulder into the semi-dark corridor. Three women stared in the direction of my office. A man with bushy hair hurried towards us. He wore a black, corduroy sport coat and a red bow tie. He rushed into my office.

"Lorraine. What's wrong? What's the problem?"

She collapsed and fell to the floor. I let go of her wrists, but I made sure her landing was soft.

Sprawled out on the floor, Lorraine sobbed uncontrollably. Her head jerked up and down. Her face turned red. She clenched her fists.

"Jerry," she said. "He did it again. He did it again." She repeated the phrase several times.

I assumed Jerry was Gerald Franklin, the attorney who owned the collection agency where Lorraine worked. He frowned at me. I shrugged my shoulders.

"You have to excuse Lorraine," he said. "She hasn't been feeling well lately. I hope she didn't cause you any real trouble, Mr. Corral."

"What's wrong with her? She thinks I did something to her. That never happened. I hope you know that."

Franklin bent over and helped Lorraine get to her feet. He spoke softly to her, urging her to stand up and then to walk to their office. He finally got her moving. She walked ahead of him. He stopped at the doorway and looked back at me.

"I really am sorry, Mr. Corral. And Lorraine will be, too, when she gets herself together. Like I said, she has some health issues. She has an appointment tomorrow with her therapist. Just in time, I'd say. I am sorry. We both are."

He puttered after Lorraine until they reached their office. He looked back at me, waved and tried to smile. I waved back at him. I wasn't smiling.

It wasn't quite ten o'clock.

෨෨ ෨෨ ෨෨

I finished Tuesday's work. No more visitors showed up unexpectedly. A few new clients contacted me for appointments, and a few checks showed up in the mail for finished jobs. I drank more coffee than I should have. It looked like I was back to the slow grind, but no complaints from me. I needed a bit of normal, and I wouldn't look down on boring.

Around four in the afternoon, I heard the attorney, Franklin, walking Lorraine out of their office. He talked in soothing tones and urged her to drink her tea. They shuffled down the hallway to the elevator. When I was sure they were gone, I opened my office door and checked out the hallway. I returned to my desk and decided to call it a day.

My phone rang. Corrine.

"You hear the news?" my sister asked.

"Been in my office all day. What's up?"

"The guy killed in Colorado Springs? You know about that?"

"Yeah, the I-25 shooter. Upped his game. They catch him?"

"No, nothing like that. The guy who was shot. They've been reporting that he was a restaurant owner, that his name was Don Allen. Yeah, you know, the ex-cop Alito—the guy Leo wanted to confront. It had to be Leo. He killed him, Gus. He's the shooter."

"I doubt that."

"It's too much of a coincidence. Alito is shot? *Now?*"

"I meant, he killed Alito, no doubt, but he's not the I-25 shooter."

"There's a difference?"

"Think about it. Has he tried to contact you?"

"I haven't heard from Leo since he stood us up and disappeared. Why would he call me?"

"Just a hunch. I'll stop by your place. We need to talk."

"I can't tonight. I have a meeting. Let's try tomorrow? After work?"

"See you then."

"Okay. I gotta go. I'm late, and now someone's at the door."

"Don't . . . " She hung up before I could finish.

On the way home, I stopped at the big burrito place, the one with the ever-changing mural on the outside of the building, and bought a bean and rice with *chicharrones,* medium *chile.* I ate it with a Dos Equis Amber and burped for the rest of the night. I tried watching the Rockies on TV, but their starting pitcher gave up three runs in the first, two more in the second, and then a grand slam in the fourth. Kino came up to bat twice with runners on second and third. He made the last out in each of those innings without driving in any runs. I fell asleep in my recliner with the game on.

A phone call around midnight woke me up. I was a little disoriented, especially when I saw the replay of a college lacrosse match on my TV. I reached for my beer and swallowed the last drink. Kino Machaco greeted me when I answered my buzzing phone.

"Gus. Sorry to call so late. I just got to our hotel here in San Francisco. *¿Cómo estás?* You have a minute?"

"Sure, Kino. Tough game tonight."

"The *pinche* Giants. I never have a good game in this damn city. Can't wait to get out of here, back home."

"What's up? You need me for something else?"

He mumbled something that was incoherent. He caught himself and raised his voice. "*Mira,* Gus. I know we're talking on Thursday, at Sardo's office. You want to talk with me, no problem. But can we meet, you and me, maybe before or after? I want to talk to you. *Only you.*"

"This got anything to do with Cuba and Hoochie?"

"Maybe. I don't know yet, not for sure. If we talk it out, you can set me straight. It's bugging me, *hombre.* Got to get it together. Can you do that?"

He sounded tired, drained of all energy. I put most of that on the fact that he'd just finished nine losing innings of major league baseball, but there was something else going on with him.

"Sure. Tell me where and when."

I hadn't wanted Sardo and Marita in the meeting when I set it up with the agent. One-on-one with Kino was perfect.

We made plans to meet at my office at seven-thirty, Thursday night. Kino thought our talk would take only a few minutes. Afterwards, he would drive me to Sardo's office. I agreed, and we finished the call. Then I tried to get back to sleep.

# - Chapter 26 -
## WEDNESDAY'S CHILD

Mid-morning Wednesday, my eyes and brain were focused on an affidavit for a lawsuit against a sham online financial adviser. Gerald Franklin, debt collection attorney, strolled into my office. He surprised me, and I jumped a bit when I realized someone else was in the office.

I couldn't help but think that even I had better taste in clothes, and my preferred outfit consisted of sweat pants and a T-shirt, so that was saying something. He had given up on the bow tie and replaced it with a bulky turtleneck sweater that he wore under yet another corduroy sport coat, this one gray. The coat was too small for him *and* the sweater, and he looked like he might pop open around the temples.

"I want to apologize again . . ." he began.

"No need. I get it. Lorraine has some issues. No harm done. I can take name-calling. Sticks and stones."

"You're handling it well, Mr. Corral. Thank you."

"My sisters have dealt with bullshit from men their entire lives. I try to remember how they were hurt, and I hope I don't come off as stupid as those men."

The first time I acted like a gorilla around a girl, when I was thirteen, Corrine spent about an hour with me. When she finished talking, and that's all she did, I was in tears, but I'd learned a lesson.

"She okay?" I asked.

Franklin tilted his head like he wasn't sure. "I should explain." He didn't have to, but I didn't stop him. "Lorraine's been under the care of a doctor for several years. I was a friend of her father's. I worked for him right after law school. He taught me all that I never learned at the university about the real practice of law. He even helped me set up my business. He was a magnanimous soul, charitable and intelligent and willing to assist a kid who had no clue. He was a good father. The least I could do was give her a job when she needed it. She *had* been doing quite well. But now . . ."

"She at home?"

"No. Her doctor has a facility, in Boulder, near the foothills. It's peaceful and the care is top notch. She's there now. She may be there for a while, or she might snap out of it soon. It's hard to say."

"Did I do anything to cause her to, uh, to relapse?"

His eyes moved over me and then over my grubby office. "I'm sure you didn't, Mr. Corral. You were in the wrong place at the wrong time."

He shook his head. "None of this is your fault."

That was an arrangement with which I was very familiar. Almost the story of my entire life.

"The way you're talking . . ." I said. "Her father's dead?"

He nodded. He patted the pockets of his coat until he found his imitation leather pocket calendar.

"I have to leave." He looked up. "But to answer your question, yes, Lorraine's father, Carl Winston, is dead, and so are her mother and brother. They were killed by a drunk driver on their way home from a restaurant where they'd celebrated Lorraine's twelfth birthday. It happened near County Line Road, when there were still empty stretches of land out there. Lorraine's leg was broken, and she couldn't walk, couldn't move. She was in considerable pain, spent the night in a ditch on the side of the road with her dead mother and brother, and her dying father. He suffered all night long until he died, at sunrise, just before someone saw the wreck and called the police. She wasn't the same after that."

"No one could be."

"Absolutely."

"So, you take care of her, like a guardian?"

"At one time I was her legal guardian. But that's not the situation any more. I simply help her when I can."

"You gave her a job, and she seemed to be doing fine for the past six months. You gave her a chance. Sounds like you still are her guardian."

He smiled. Dumb clothes or not, and regardless of what I thought about the business he was in, I had to give props to Gerald Franklin.

He walked back to his office. At his door he pulled a pipe out of a pocket and struggled to light it.

"Of course," I thought.

The rest of the day flashed by with a torrent of phone calls, last minute requests for service of process and walk-ins who had no business talking to a private investigator. And no business *for* a private investigator.

By the end of eight hours at the office, I was strung out on caffeine and sugar. Too many candy bars, bear claws and Nutty Buddies. I thought I'd find a place where I could have a real meal, with salad, vegetables and beer, but that would have to wait until after I talked with Corrine.

To get to Corrine's house on the Northside, I had to drive through the thick of Denver traffic, no matter which route I chose. Rush hour had begun, and it took me almost a half-hour.

On the way, I turned the dial of the radio, hoping for something different. I stopped channel surfing when I heard Nina Simone moaning pain and anger.

*Ain't it hard just to live? Just to live.*

I'd landed on the jazz station. The song was about gritty Baltimore, but it came right at me, the melancholy Mexican, trying to hang on in Mile High Denver. The song ended and I snapped back.

I turned the dial again and listened to the news. One story was repeated, several times. Police had responded to a 911 call from a woman in the Lower Highlands neighborhood who said an intruder had broken in and now held her at gunpoint. I gunned the pickup and cursed the traffic.

☽ ☽ ☽

I had to park several blocks away from Corrine's house. The police had cordoned off a perimeter. I talked to five cops and showed my I.D. a dozen times before I finally made it to the officer in charge. Police cruisers lined the street in front of my sister's house. Men with scoped weapons leaned on the cars, their weapons aimed at the house. At least three snipers were on roofs across from Corrine's.

Captain Leonard Garth listened politely as I told him I was the hostage's brother and that I knew the man with the gun. Then he told me to stay out of the way.

Garth used a bullhorn to try to communicate with Hudgens. He repeatedly asked to speak with Leo. Apparently, they'd figured out he was the man in Corrine's house. Garth played on Hudgens' past as a fellow cop.

"You don't want to hurt any of these people, right? They're your brothers and sisters. You worked the streets with these men and women."

No one responded.

I tried to get him to let me use the bullhorn.

"I know this guy," I said. "I can get him to release my sister."

"Shut up and get back or I'll have you arrested."

He waved the bullhorn at me, and I had no doubt he'd hit me with it if he thought it would help the situation.

I felt helpless, useless. But I reminded myself that Corrine was a tough cookie. Our mother gave her that nickname the first time Corrine fell off her bike, broke her arm and didn't shed any tears.

I repeated to myself: "Corrine will be okay."

Garth ordered his men to "make this asshole go away," meaning me. Two uniforms pushed me behind the crime scene tape. In their minds I was just part of the crowd of onlookers. I craned my neck, but I couldn't see much except Garth and his entourage, and Corrine's front door.

That's when the door opened. All the cops noticeably stiffened. Guns were turned to the doorway. No one spoke, and it looked like no one breathed.

Leo Hudgens emerged with his hands up. Blood covered his face. Corrine walked behind him. She also had her hands pointed at the sky.

"Drop to the ground!" Garth shouted through his bullhorn. "Drop to the ground!" he shouted again. "Drop all weapons. Drop to the ground!"

Corrine lowered herself to her knees. Hudgens looked to his right and left. He made a sudden movement towards the street. Corrine grabbed him by the ankle and tripped him. He fell face first onto Corrine's brown lawn. Several cops jumped him and held him down. Another cop aimed his handgun at Corrine's head.

When she was finally able to tell her story, it was obvious that Hudgens had hoped that the Denver police would kill him. His wish had come damn close to being granted.

Hudgens had convinced Corrine to let him into her house. She still held onto hope for him. Once inside, he pulled his gun and forced her to call the police. He told Corrine that he'd tracked Alito for days, figured out his routine and mapped the best place to ambush him.

"Alito ruined my life," he said to Corrine. "And I finished his."

He prepared to rush the cops surrounding the house. Corrine surprised him with a vase across the top of his head. He dropped his gun and she pounced on it. She made him walk outside with his hands up. Then she placed the gun on a chair and followed Hudgens.

"I didn't want to step through the door with a gun in my hand," she said. "In case one of the cops was trigger-happy."

Hudgens was taken away. Corrine was offered a ride to the hospital for an exam, as well as counseling for the emotional trauma. She declined both offers. Captain Garth eventually thanked her for preventing further bloodshed.

"You saved Hudgens' life," he said. "That scum will never appreciate that. But you also prevented possible harm to my officers. You're a brave lady, Ms. Corral."

Corrine blushed. She and Garth scheduled an appointment at the district office for her to make an official statement.

"This fellow says he's your brother." He pointed at me like I was a goiter on a pig's neck. "That right?"

"Never saw him before," she said.

Garth straightened up as though he was a hunting dog sniffing out a squirrel. I waited for Corrine to laugh it off. And waited.

# Chapter 27
## CIEN AÑOS

It was well after midnight before Corrine, Max and I were the only people in Corrine's house. Thursday morning. Max rushed over when she saw Corrine's face on TV, but she had to wait with us outside until the crime scene and forensics crews finished their jobs and cleared the house. When we finally sat at the kitchen table, Max and Corrine shared a bottle of white wine, and I helped myself to the six pack of Pacifico in the fridge.

"How could he do that to you?" Max asked. "You tried to help him. You picked him up out of the gutter. Then he comes after you with a gun?"

Max liked to say, "The weekend begins on Thursday." She was the leader of a punk/grunge/rap/retro all-girl band, so she had to say stuff like that. So far, the weekend had been a bummer.

Sweet, chilled-out Maxine was pissed. She had patience for just about anything except a threat to her family. Then her Chicana roots came out, loud and angry.

"He was desperate," Corrine said. "He wouldn't have hurt me. He needed an excuse for the cops to show up in force. He wanted to end it. For himself, not me."

"You trust him more than I do," I said. "I would've shot the motherfucker if I had the chance."

"I would have helped you, Gus," Max said.

Corrine smiled at that. She must've been thinking of all the times she had come to our rescue, especially during our teenage years when, more than once, she'd saved our asses from whichever bully was tormenting Max, or whatever hoodlum was trying to prove he was a man by beating me up.

"Look," she said, "*gracias,* and all that, but it's over, none of us got hurt, and hopefully Leo will get some help. He's gonna have a hard time in prison."

"That's what you're worried about?" I asked.

"You know what it's gonna be like, Gus. He might not last long."

"Between you and me, I hope he ends up in the same joint as Delly Thomas. That'd be justice."

She shook her head. "I'm no friend of dirty cops. I knew Hudgens when he was a decent man. I want to think that decency is still there. I think he deserves a second chance, we all do, sooner or later. That's all I'm saying."

"He's killed at least twice. They may pin all the highway shootings on him. He'll be lucky if he doesn't end up on death row. His second chances have run out."

Corrine frowned at my words.

"I'll give him this much," I said. "He took care of Alito."

"You found Alito for him, right?" Max asked. "That gonna be trouble for you?"

I hadn't thought of that possibility. "Well, technically, Soapy found Alito."

Corrine slapped my wrist.

"But we haven't done anything illegal, although the cops may stir something up."

"Leo won't burn you," Corrine said.

Max and I looked at each other.

"If you say so, sis," Max said. "I hope you know this guy like you think you do."

We didn't say anything for several minutes. I stood up and walked to Corrine's kitchen window. The ash and elm trees in her backyard were spotlighted by the bright, full moon. Branches glowed as if they were wired for light. The patchy hedge undulated like a metallic rug, woven of silver and gold. It reminded me of the Cuban night from a hundred years ago.

Corrine turned on her record player and placed an LP on the turntable. Wouldn't you know it: *Cien Años* by Pedro Infante. Like she read my mind.

*Me duele hasta la vida.*

Life hurts. Really?

ᘒ᠉ ᘒ᠉ ᘒ᠉

The three of us had a decent and expensive breakfast at one of the new restaurants on Thirty-second, walking distance from Corrine's. I paid for the meal, which caused mild hysteria from my sisters. No one could remember when I'd picked up the tab, including me.

"You been through hell, Corrine," I said. "It's the least I can do."

"Sounds good to me," Max said. "Club dates for Mezcla have been scarce lately."

We went our separate ways. I was bone-tired again, but I knew I couldn't sleep. I went home, showered, changed my shirt and, twenty minutes later, checked in at my office, where I picked up the newspaper in the hallway and made myself at home.

The Rockies returned to Denver on a beautiful day. They brought with them an ugly losing streak—five of their first seven games. Players and coaches talked about how good it would be to play in Coors Field. They sounded like they were ready for the All-Star break. It wasn't hard to believe that it was going to be a long season.

But the build-up to the home opener never faltered. The fan appreciation events, which began on Wednesday, were packed with hardcore season ticket holders, one-game-a-year families, autograph seekers, high school coaches and little league teams. Sports shows on TV featured taped interviews with players, the manager and fans. Baseball websites debated the good and bad points of the team's starting rotation. Twitter and Facebook were agog with the one bright spot: the lanky, pimple-faced kid from Wyoming who owned the two wins for the Rockies. He'd been rushed into the starting rotation when the designated ace stubbed his toe on a doorstop in a freak accident, and made the most of his opportunity.

There was something else. Kino's slump had become a national topic. It was so bad that oddsmakers in Las Vegas were willing to take bets on how many games would be played before Kino was benched. The odds were even that the opening home series would be his last as a starter.

Kino's photograph graced the first page of the special Rockies insert in the *Denver Post*. He wasn't smiling. The headline read: *Does Machaco Have Anything Left?* The writer speculated that Kino had burned through his talent and skills the previous year, when he almost single-handedly led the team to the World Series.

"For the good of the team *and* Kino," he wrote, "Machaco should be used off the bench. Let him end his great career with dignity, if not glory," the writer concluded.

I didn't know whether the reporter knew what he was talking about, not sure I had an opinion one way or the other. What I did know was that Kino and I had to talk, and the conversation would not help the superstar get his mojo back.

I answered a handful of messages, typed a few invoices and reports on my laptop, and then decided I needed fresh air, or at least relief from the dungeon-like atmosphere of the Lewis Building.

Instead of waiting all day in my office for my meeting with Kino, I locked up, walked the couple of blocks to my parking space, started the pickup and made my way to Speer. I exited on I-25, then, a few minutes later, exited again to I-70. I drove east, away from the city and the mountains.

Freeways work when traffic is light, and that day I drove as though I had I-70 all to myself. I sped by the Purina pet food processing plant, with its unique bouquet that nauseated people at their club level seats at Coors Field, five miles away. The battered communities of Globeville, Elyria and Swansea were barely noticeable under the arches of the elevated highway.

I drove past the Havana Street exit. I'd taken that exit a few times, involuntarily. It was the way to the county jail. The light rail rushed along the side of the highway to the airport, then I flew by the Peña Boulevard exit.

I left the industrial grime of Northeast Denver. Expanses of what was once called the "Great American Desert" stretched in early spring optimism: a bit of green, a few birds, clumps of snow—dirty and gray, but melting.

I pushed the limits of the truck on the highway. I told myself I should know what the tin can had inside, what it would give me in a pinch. And that was true, up to a point. At the heart of my lonely cruise toward the Colorado plains was my uncertainty about all that had happened in the Machaco job, and how Hudgens had ended.

The ex-cop was on his way to years of penitentiary torment and abuse. Corrine wouldn't let it go, of that I was certain. Would she drag me back into the mess of Hudgens' life?

Lourdes' letter should have closed the Machaco file. She wrapped up the loose ends quite nicely. If that wasn't enough, Marita's surprise visit should have been the capper, the last bit of theater for a case that had way too much blood and betrayal. The script had been played out, but I couldn't let the play end. Not yet.

When I stopped, I was close to the small town of Bennett, almost forty miles from Denver. I needed gas and a restroom. I found both, then headed back to the city. I'd killed two hours.

# - Chapter 28 -
## WHETHER YOU WANT IT OR NOT

I called Soapy to finalize our plans for the night meeting. She was eager and excited. Maybe she should've been the investigator and I should've been her assistant?

"You ready?" I asked.

"Absolutely. I double-checked the figures, looked again at the relevant files. It's as good as it's gonna be."

"You okay with giving this info to Kino?"

"He has a right to know. He won't like how I found it, but he needs to have it. And I finally feel sure about the whole thing."

"Then you're on for tonight."

I turned on the answering service app on my phone and walked across the street to the Blind Bat. I realized I was hungry and that the first half of the day had slipped away from me. I ordered a Dos Equis, a Jalapeño cream cheese burger and onion rings. My breakfast with my sisters had worn off, and I gobbled the bar food like it was my last meal.

When I came up for air, I ordered another beer. I thought about calling Jerome or Corrine and filling them in on what I had in mind, but why drag them into something that could be nothing at all or a real mess? I had no good answer. Besides, Soapy would be with me at the meeting. If she wasn't enough backup, then I had miscalculated. Again.

⋙ ⋙ ⋙

Sofía Santisteven walked into my office a minute or two before seven. She sniffed her nose and gave me a dirty look.

"You been drinking?"

"I had a couple beers with lunch. Big lunch."

"And then what?"

"I did some work until I was hungry again."

"So, you went back to the Bat and drank more beer?"

"I had a couple more."

"Did you eat dinner?"

"Lost my appetite."

"You shouldn't have done that. We need to think clearly. We don't know how Machaco will react."

"He'll be upset, yeah. But he's a big boy."

She shrugged. "Still gonna hurt."

"It's your show," I continued. "You got all the data. I'm just along for the ride. Anyhow, I'm not drunk, just been drinking."

"You're not funny. I hope I can count on you."

Soapy hurt my feelings. I was under control, she didn't have to worry. In fact, the beer hadn't done anything except relax me a bit. Nothing wrong with that. I was overdue on some chillin' time. Who was the boss in this partnership anyway?

"I got your back. No worry. We're doing the right thing, going beyond what anyone, including Kino, should expect."

"We should go to the police," she said.

"That's up to Kino. If he wants to handle it that way, we'll turn over the info you collected. Until he says otherwise, it stays with you and me and him."

As if on cue, the superstar knocked on the office door and walked in. He had a broad smile. His head was shinier than ever, and he still looked like he could pick me up and tear me in half.

"My man Gus!" he shouted.

He almost ran to me. He yanked me out of my chair and hugged me like a child hugs her favorite stuffed animal, with crushing intensity. I had to catch my breath when he let me go.

"I can't thank you enough," he said in rapid-fire, clipped Cuban Spanish. "You took care of the problem, you risked your life. You saved Lourdes."

I nodded and backed away.

"I can't thank you enough," he repeated in English.

I pointed at the empty chair and indicated he should sit down. Soapy stared with her mouth open. Kino had taken over the small room in a matter of seconds. The space, light and air were all his. Soapy and I just shared whatever he left for us.

I smiled back at him and debated whether we should small talk or get to it. Although he continued to grin like a clown, he couldn't sit still. He tapped his feet and fingers, twisted his trunk right and left and basically looked uncomfortable. Beads of sweat appeared on his forehead and rolled into the collar of his silk shirt. His form-fitting slacks bunched up at his thousand-dollar loafers.

Kino may have been trying to come off as under control, but the man had serious problems. He was barely holding it together.

"It's good to see you, too," I said.

Soapy's fake cough grabbed my attention.

"Kino, this is Sofía Santisteven. She works for me."

He jerked his head in her direction. I don't think he'd noticed her.

"I said I wanted to meet with only you."

"Yes, of course. But she has information for you that you will want."

He grunted. Soapy sat back in her chair.

"But first, you wanted to meet before we go to Sardo's office. What's up?"

Kino leaned forward, almost stretching his neck over my desk.

"If you say this girl is okay, then she can stay. If she doesn't respect me and my business, she will be sorry."

"This girl understands perfectly," Soapy said. "You don't have to be concerned with me. I'm working *for* you."

"You're in big trouble if you mess me up," he warned.

"*No te preocupes. Estoy de tu lado.*"

Her perfect Spanish caught him off-guard. He took a deep breath.

"*Como dije,*" Kino said, "I'm grateful for what you've already done, Gus. It was more than either of us expected. You risked your life. Lourdes tells me you are a good man, a strong man. That's all I need to know about you."

I burped beer. He didn't seem to notice.

"The thing is . . . I'm worried about Ben, my agent. We have been together since I came to the States. He's helped me in all kinds of ways. He's been there for me *and* Alberto. I think of him as a friend as well as my agent."

"But something's wrong?" I asked.

His face collapsed like a dead balloon. His anguish covered his words and I found myself leaning towards him.

"I think he's stealing from me," he said. "He's the one with access to everything I own, everything I have. There have been problems, questions. My accountant started my taxes. He says he can't understand what happened to a million dollars. Can you believe that? How can a million dollars be lost? How can this happen?"

Soapy and I looked at each other. Kino had beaten us to the punch. We were ready to tell him the same thing. His money didn't add up, and someone close, like Ben Sardo, was ripping him off. Soapy estimated that over the past five years, more than three million dollars had been siphoned from Kino's accounts. Apparently, his accountant hadn't dug deep enough yet. Or maybe he was in on it with the agent, misdirecting him with one million so they could make off with the other two.

"We have to tell you something," I said. "It's the truth, and you need to hear it, whether you want it or not."

For the next twenty minutes, Soapy and I explained all that we knew about his money, and how we knew it. We laid out spreadsheets, email messages and bank statements. Soapy did most of the talking. I didn't understand everything about how she'd found the information, and neither did Kino. It didn't matter.

When Kino first hired me, Soapy hacked into his various accounts held by banks, financial advisers, Sardo and Kino himself. Kino had approved me looking at his finances. I told him I needed a complete picture of the Machaco brothers, just in case there was more to what I was walking into than a straightforward payment of overdue gambling debts. Soapy got in and kept following a trail of misplaced money even after I returned from Cuba. That was on her own initiative, and illegal, but I kept that to myself.

We told him that it looked like Sardo was the thief, and that's why I wanted to meet at his office. I would tell Sardo what we knew, with Kino present, let him defend himself, and then Kino could decide what to do. His options were to turn Sardo over to the cops or simply fire him and move on. It was entirely up to Kino. I also thought for a second that another option was for Kino to hurt Sardo, but I kept that to myself, too.

By the time we finished, Kino had finally eased up on his clenched fists and jaw. The news from us appeared to calm him down. I guessed he felt better knowing that the discrepancies he saw weren't only in his imagination, and that he wasn't paranoid. There actually *was* something wrong.

"We're late," Soapy said.

We picked up the paperwork, turned out the lights and followed Kino out of the building and into the street. We climbed into his low-slung Porsche.

Jerome would've had a tricky time sitting in Kino's ride. I could barely believe it—I was actually wrapping up a job where I didn't need Jerome's special skill set. I was grateful for that.

# - Chapter 29 -
## GRATITUDE

The night guard at the skyscraper where Ben Sardo had his office knew Kino on sight. As soon as he saw us he opened the building doors. He smiled like he'd won the lottery. He must've said, "Anything you need, Mr. Kino," at least a dozen times before he finally used a key to call an elevator for us.

Sardo's suite of offices was on the nineteenth floor. When we exited the elevator, glass, chrome and leather surrounded us. Lights from other downtown buildings reflected off metallic corners of coffee tables, chairs and desks. Photos of heroes of every professional American sport hung on the walls. The place smelled like money and promises of *even* more money.

We found Sardo in his corner office, down a long hall and out of sight of the oversized reception desk in the suite entrance.

Sardo's business space was filled with display cabinets, bookshelves and framed memorabilia on the walls. Chrome and black leather chairs were spread around the room. Off to one side sat a short leather couch.

The cabinets held trophies, signed baseballs and souvenirs such as tickets and VIP passes. The books on the shelves were about pro sports or making money in pro sports. A black baseball bat sitting on a mahogany shelf contained numerous autographs in silver Sharpie. Hanging on one wall was a string of eight by tens of the biggest names in baseball adorned with notes of gratitude made out to "Ben" or "B.S."

On the wall behind Sardo hung a chrome frame that held thirty-two baseball cards, four rows of eight. A brass plate attached to the bottom of the frame was engraved with the words *1956 Topps Hall of Famers.* I recognized Willie Mays, Mickey Mantle, Roberto

Clemente. The cards looked new and shiny, but they were more than sixty years old.

Ben Sardo sat behind a green-glass desk that was as big as a pool table. He wore pressed black jeans, black running shoes and a crimson Harvard Law School sweatshirt. The buttoned-down collar of a white shirt with blue pinstripes peeked over the neck.

He was on the phone.

"Sure, send them up," he said before he hung up and saw us.

The agent turned on his electric smile. "Joaquín!" he shouted. "Man is it good to see you." He stood and opened his arms to greet his client with a big hug.

Machaco walked up to his agent, stared at him for a few seconds, then he punched the agent in the nose with a swift powerful jab from his right hand. Sardo fell to his knees. His eyes rolled up and down. Blood leaked out of his nose and across the H of his sweatshirt. He looked at Kino with a cockeyed grin. His hand stretched up to Kino. It trembled like the last leaf on the branch. Kino pushed away Sardo's arm. The agent fell forward, out.

"What the hell!" Soapy hollered.

"Jesus!" was what I managed to say.

Soapy and I knelt beside Sardo. He wasn't dead, but his nose looked seriously injured. I tried to slow down the bleeding with a monogrammed handkerchief I found in the back pocket of his jeans.

Sardo groaned and mumbled, but he stayed unconscious.

Meanwhile, Kino strutted around the office, swearing in Spanish and kicking things like Sardo's chair and a shiny silver wastebasket. He knocked over a cabinet, ripped photos off the wall.

"Calm down," Soapy repeatedly told him.

It was no use. Joaquín Machaco was angry, and he kept looking for things on which to vent that anger.

"What happened?"

Soapy and I turned to the voice. Alberto Machaco and Marita Valdés stood in the doorway.

Kino stopped pacing.

"That son of a bitch!" he shouted. "That punk! *¡Robándome!* After all I've done for him! This is how he pays me back!"

Alberto grabbed Kino's arm. He draped his arms around his brother's shoulders.

"What is going on, *hermano*? What are you talking about? What happened to Ben?"

"They can tell you." Kino pointed at Soapy and me. "They have the proof."

That was our cue. Soapy unrolled her documents and spread them on Sardo's desk. Alberto and Kino stood next to the desk, Marita moved back a few feet.

I had expected Marita. Alberto was a surprise, although his presence made sense. He was part of the family, Kino's partner.

I kept the handkerchief on Sardo's nose, but it was soaked with his blood. Bruises were starting to ring his eyes. While Soapy meticulously arranged her presentation, I called 911 and asked for an ambulance.

I listened to Soapy describe how she unearthed the uncounted money, and how Sardo must have masked his fees and expenses to hide his trail. Alberto asked questions, cursed Sardo and tried to calm down his brother whenever Kino worked himself into another rage.

I sat on the floor. Relief tried to work its way through my system. I took a few deep breaths and thought I should look for a towel for Sardo. His handkerchief was ruined, useless.

I turned to Marita, to ask her to help me look.

She held a small pistol in her hands. The gun was pointed at all of us.

# - Chapter 30 -
## SANGRE

"Put that away," I said.

Marita turned the gun directly at me. "Stay out of this, Gus. This is not your problem."

"What is this, Marí?" Kino asked. He shook off his brother and walked towards Marita. "What have you done?"

Alberto faltered, as if his legs had lost their strength. He followed Kino, but he didn't say anything.

"Give me the gun, Marí," Kino said.

He reached out to her. She twisted the gun and pulled the trigger. Soapy screamed. The glass in the baseball card display exploded; shards landed at my feet, by my hands, on Sardo. Several of the cards flew into the air, then floated to the ground. A few dropped in Sardo's blood.

Kino staggered backwards. He and Alberto stood next to one another, their mouths shut in tight narrow frowns, fists clenched.

"At last, *al fin*," Marí said. "I have you both."

"For what?" I asked.

I was still on my knees, trying to deal with Sardo.

"Poor Gus. The truth is right here, in this room. Can't you see it?"

She held the gun on the Machaco brothers.

Alberto stepped forward. "Give me the gun, Marí. You don't know what you're doing."

He reached for the gun. Marita pulled the trigger again.

I shouted, "No!"

The bullet hit Alberto in the shoulder. He spun around and collapsed on the short leather couch.

Marita froze. She studied the gun in her hands as though she didn't know what it was.

Kino roared. He jumped on Marita, knocked the gun away and threw her to the ground. He pulled back his fist to strike her.

Soapy and I shouted, "No! No!"

He looked at us and sat back on his haunches. Alberto twisted and turned on the now bloody couch.

"You fool," Marita said. "You're still protecting him, still acting like his older brother, even after all he's done to you. He's your blood, *tu sangre*, but that's not enough. Blood can betray."

Kino looked at his wounded brother. Blood dripped from Kino's left hand. I guessed he'd cut himself on a piece of glass when he trashed the office.

"You shielded him in Cuba, when he pushed Claudio to his death," Marita continued, sounding out-of-breath. "You took the blame because you knew nothing would happen to you. You were the rising star, the future. Alberto would have gone to prison. Even Miguel thought you killed his brother."

"That's history, Marita. You knew the truth all along but never told Hoochie. You covered for Alberto as much as me, as much as anyone."

Alberto groaned.

"Alberto needs an ambulance," Kino said.

"He can die," Marita said.

"Don't listen to her," Alberto said between groans. "She's crazy, always has been, you know that." He staggered his words.

I agreed with Alberto. There was something off about the woman. I stood up. My hands were covered with Sardo's blood and I stepped in Alberto's blood when I moved.

Marita also stood up. Her legs were smeared with red. One of her shoes had fallen off her foot. Whatever happened, no one was getting away clean. Not this time.

Marita laughed. "Am I crazy to tell you that Alberto's been stealing from you for years? Am I crazy to say that he was the one who tried to steal the payoff to Miguel? That he brought me in his plan because he knew I wanted to hurt Miguel? That he is the one responsible for Miguel's death, for the burning of Lourdes' house, the death of Sánchez? For all of it. Ask him, Joaquín. Let him deny it now."

Alberto struggled to sit up on the slick couch.

"She's lying. There's no way. It's impossible. Remember that I was shot at in Cuba. Am I responsible for that too?"

"That was the incompetents you hired," Marita said. "They made mistakes all through your goddamn plan."

Kino stared at Alberto. His hands shook. White flecks appeared on the corners of his mouth.

Alberto slid further towards the floor.

"It's not like she's putting it," Alberto said. "She's trying to trick you, Joaquín."

Alberto's panicked voice could barely be heard in the wrecked office. Even though we were hundreds of feet above the ground, in an airtight, weather-proof building, the noise of the city leaked into the room. An ambulance's wail mixed with police sirens, car honks and shrill bus brakes.

The phone on Sardo's desk rang but no one picked it up.

Kino glared at his brother. "The truth. *La verdad.* What is it?"

Alberto's words came out faster, more urgent. "Look, it wasn't me. She is the one who wanted to steal from Hoochie. She dragged me into her scheme. It was *her* idea—I had no choice. She threatened to tell Hoochie the truth about Claudio. He would've come after me. He would've known that I pushed Claudio into the car. He would have killed me. You know that, Joaquín. I had no choice."

"Miguel wasn't supposed to die!" Marita screamed. "You destroyed everything. I only wanted the money, to punish him, to make him pay for how he treated me. He wasn't supposed to pay with his life."

She choked on her sobs. Tears streamed down her face. She fell limp against the wall.

Kino stumbled backwards.

I looked at Soapy. "Alberto?"

"I didn't go far enough," Soapy said, her voice weak. "We thought it was Sardo, so that's what I looked for. The accounts are mixed up. Complicated. It could be Alberto." She shook her head. "I'm sorry. I missed it."

"Stealing from me for years wasn't enough?" Kino growled. He zeroed in on Alberto. "You had to have the money that was to pay off your debt? You had to have it all?"

"No, Kino. It's not like she says. She's ill, crazy, she's always been crazy. She . . . "

Kino threw a punch at Alberto, but he missed. He fell backwards and landed on his side. Alberto moved off the couch. He stood over Kino.

"You have everything!" he screamed. "More than you will ever need. You didn't miss what I took. All these years, you didn't know. How much do you need? How much?"

Kino jumped to his feet and smashed his fist into Alberto's throat. Alberto gagged and rolled to the floor. Kino yanked the autographed bat from its perch on the shelf.

Soapy screamed. She grabbed Kino's arm. He shook her off and slammed her against one of the bookcases. She groaned, tried to stand but fell back to the floor.

I heard the elevator chime, then the elevator doors open. Men shouted, and several people rushed through the office halls.

"Police! Police! Everyone on the floor!"

Through the glass walls and the high-rise windows, Denver's neon and fluorescent night sparkled like gilded costume jewelry.

I jumped on Kino's back and pounded his ribs. He tried to shake me off, but I clung to his body. He twisted, grunted and cursed. My bloody hands lost their grip and when he turned in a complete circle I tumbled off him.

I struggled to a squatting position as I tried to find my balance. He jerked the bat and smashed my forehead. It felt like an icepick pierced my brain. I couldn't hear anything, my hands went numb, my eyesight blurred. I tried to hold on to the desk, but my fingers slipped and I tipped over. I couldn't move, couldn't feel my legs. Blood flowed into my eyes, my mouth.

"Drop the bat!" someone shouted.

Kino gripped the bat with both hands, raised it over his head and swung it at Alberto's face.

I drifted into darkness.